ANN M. MA

THE BABY-SITTERS CLUB

THE TRUTH ABOUT STACEY

A GRAPHIC NOVEL BY
RAINA TELGEMEIER
WITH COLOR BY BRADEN LAMB

graphix

An Imprint of

■SCHOLASTIC

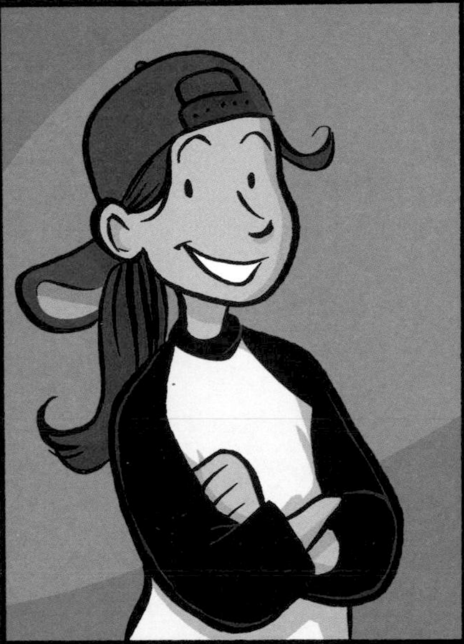

KRISTY THOMAS
PRESIDENT

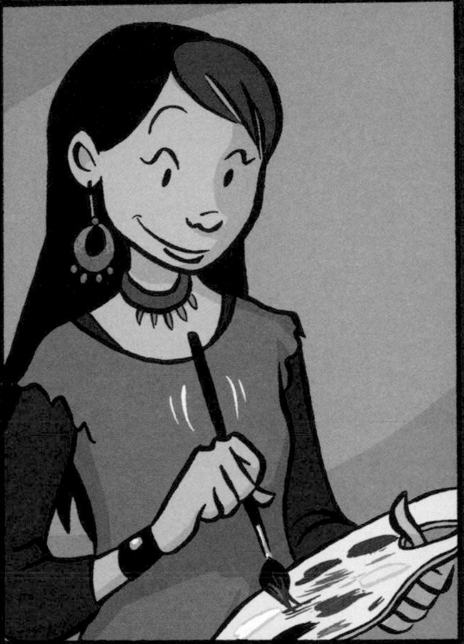

CLAUDIA KISHI
VICE PRESIDENT

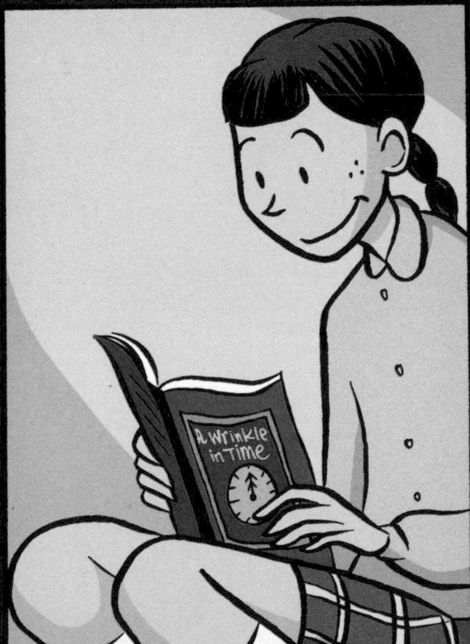
A Wrinkle in Time

MARY ANNE SPIER
SECRETARY

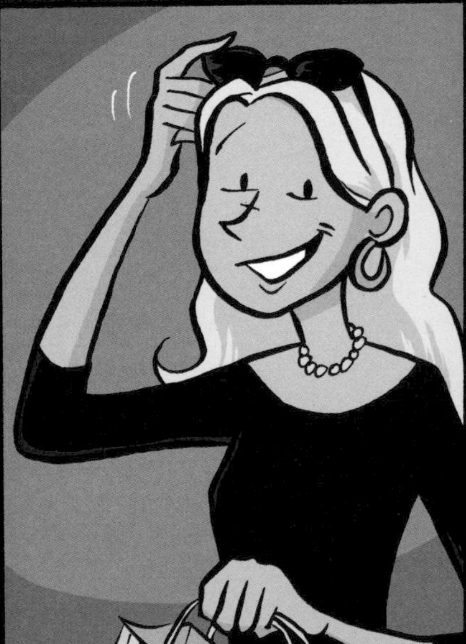

STACEY MCGILL
TREASURER

CHAPTER 1

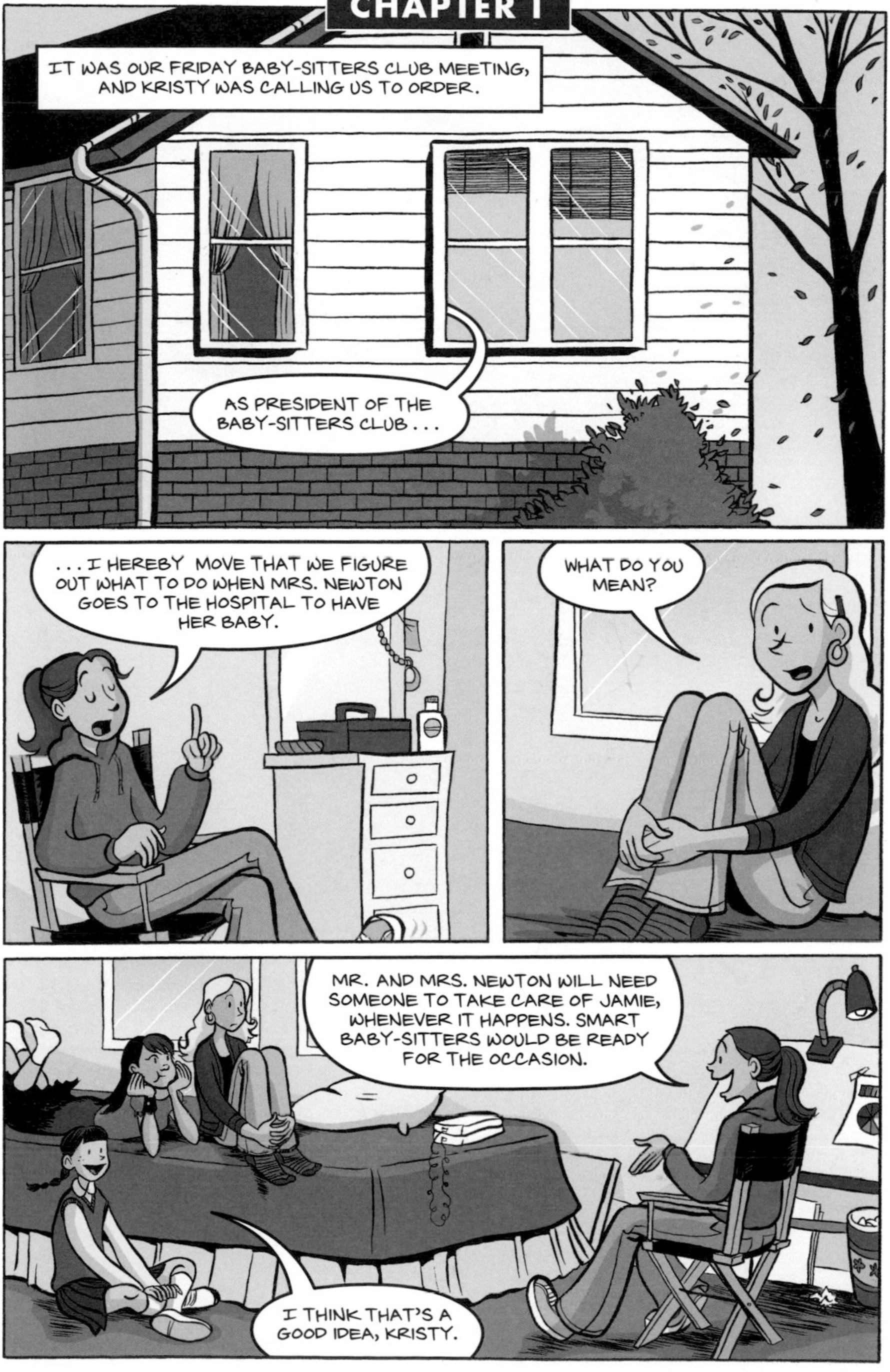

IT WAS OUR FRIDAY BABY-SITTERS CLUB MEETING, AND KRISTY WAS CALLING US TO ORDER.
AS PRESIDENT OF THE BABY-SITTERS CLUB . . .
. . . I HEREBY MOVE THAT WE FIGURE OUT WHAT TO DO WHEN MRS. NEWTON GOES TO THE HOSPITAL TO HAVE HER BABY.
WHAT DO YOU MEAN?
MR. AND MRS. NEWTON WILL NEED SOMEONE TO TAKE CARE OF JAMIE, WHENEVER IT HAPPENS. SMART BABY-SITTERS WOULD BE READY FOR THE OCCASION.
I THINK THAT'S A GOOD IDEA, KRISTY.

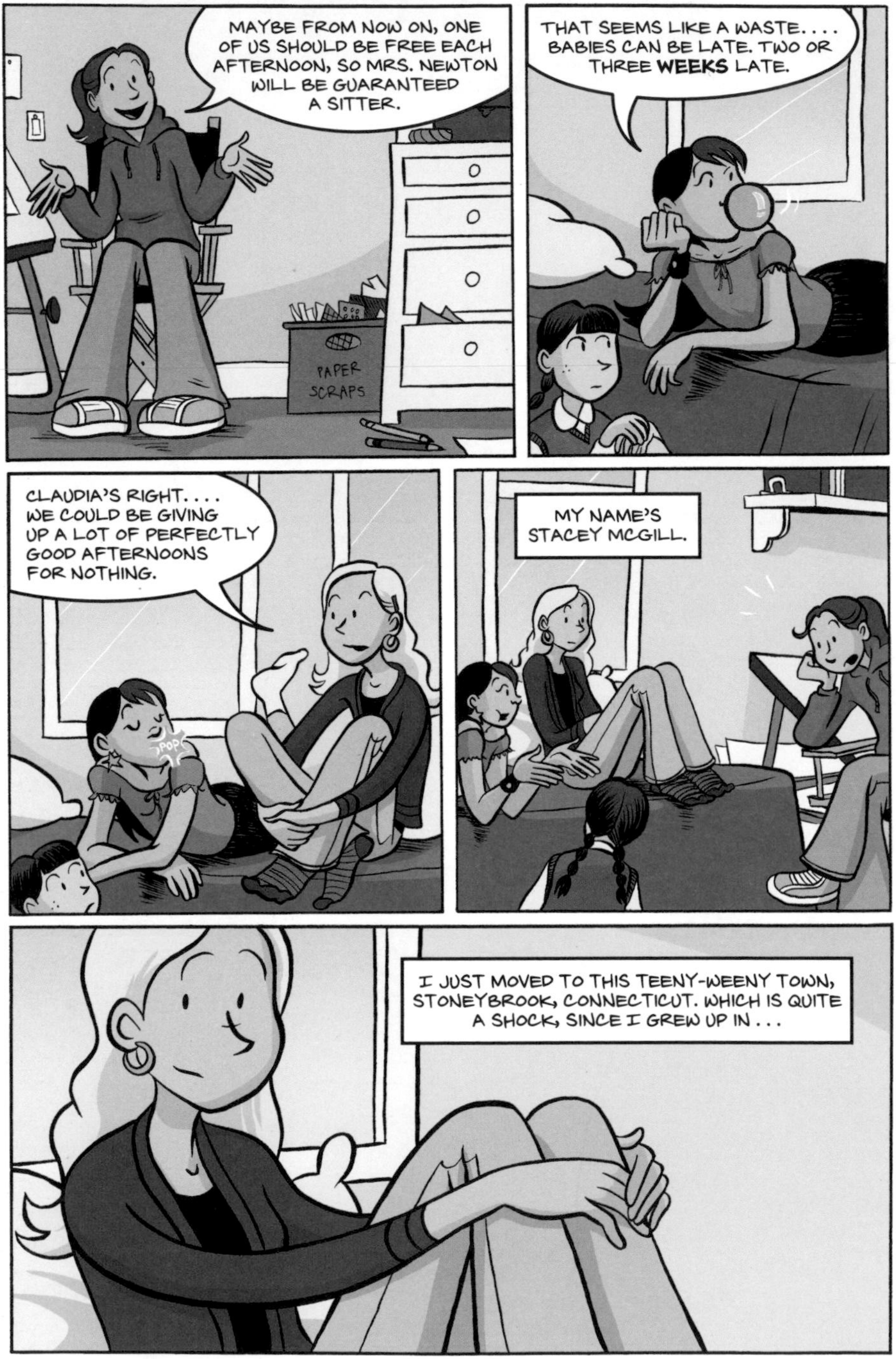
MAYBE FROM NOW ON, ONE OF US SHOULD BE FREE EACH AFTERNOON, SO MRS. NEWTON WILL BE GUARANTEED A SITTER.
PAPER SCRAPS
THAT SEEMS LIKE A WASTE. . . . BABIES CAN BE LATE. TWO OR THREE **WEEKS** LATE.
CLAUDIA'S RIGHT. . . . WE COULD BE GIVING UP A LOT OF PERFECTLY GOOD AFTERNOONS FOR NOTHING.
POP
MY NAME'S STACEY MCGILL.
I JUST MOVED TO THIS TEENY-WEENY TOWN, STONEYBROOK, CONNECTICUT. WHICH IS QUITE A SHOCK, SINCE I GREW UP IN . . .

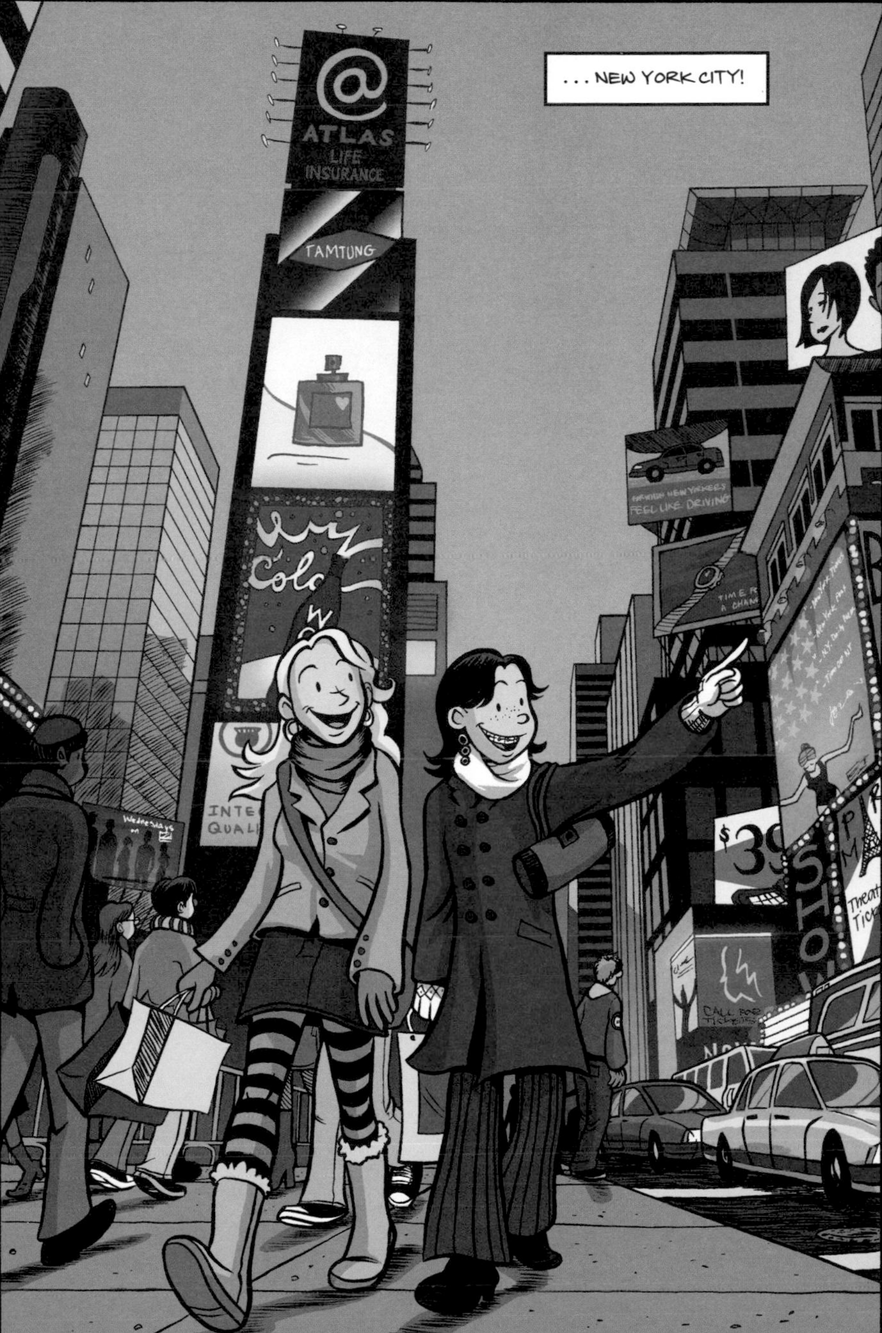
. . . NEW YORK CITY!
ATLAS
LIFE
INSURANCE
TAMTUNG
FEEL LIKE DRIVING

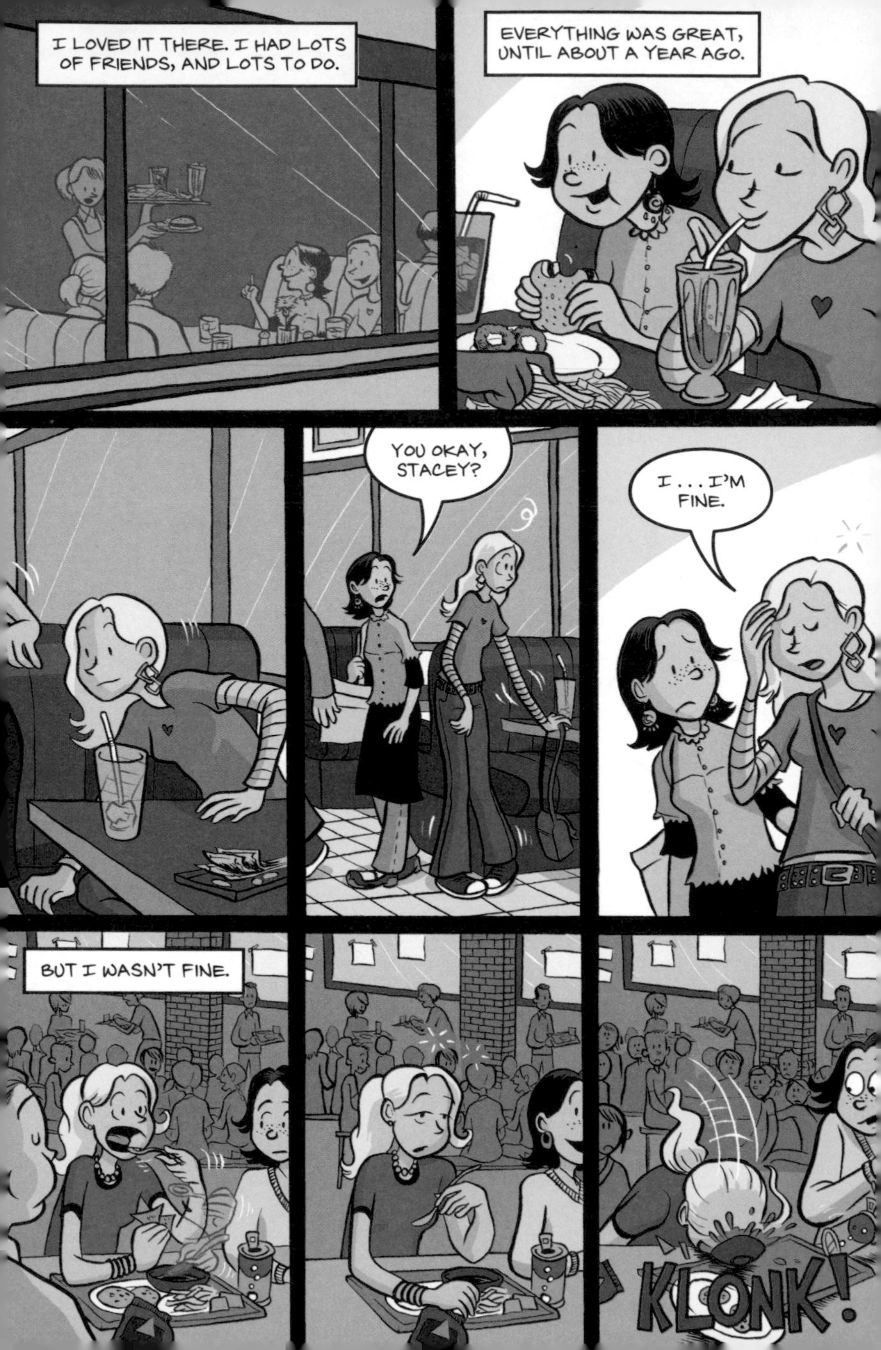
I LOVED IT THERE. I HAD LOTS OF FRIENDS, AND LOTS TO DO.
EVERYTHING WAS GREAT, UNTIL ABOUT A YEAR AGO.
YOU OKAY, STACEY?
I . . . I'M FINE.
BUT I WASN'T FINE.
KLONK!

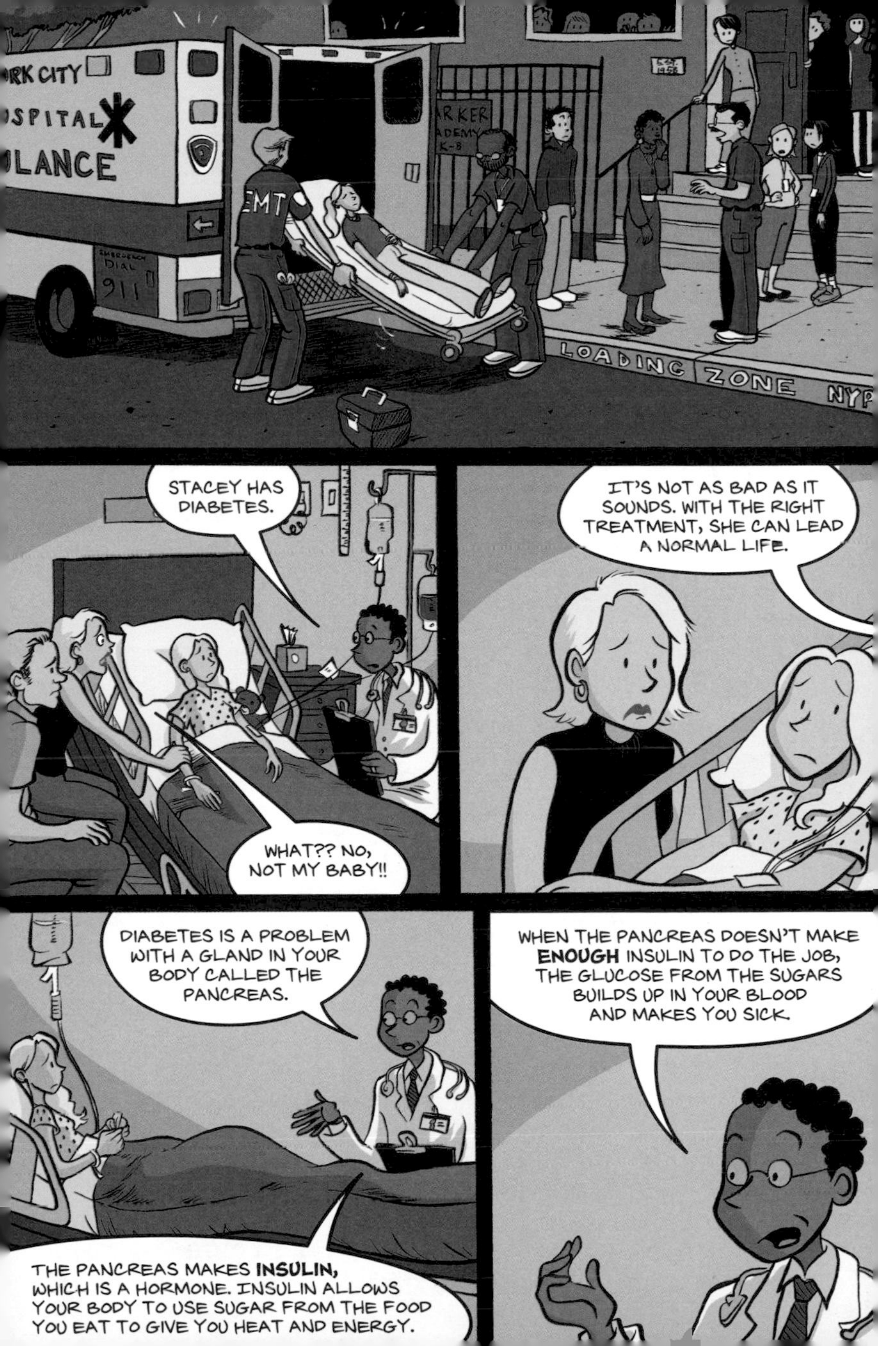

RK CITY
SPITAL
LANCE
EMT
DIAL 911
ARKER
ADEMY
K-8
LOADING ZONE NYP
STACEY HAS DIABETES.
WHAT?? NO, NOT MY BABY!!
IT'S NOT AS BAD AS IT SOUNDS. WITH THE RIGHT TREATMENT, SHE CAN LEAD A NORMAL LIFE.
DIABETES IS A PROBLEM WITH A GLAND IN YOUR BODY CALLED THE PANCREAS.
THE PANCREAS MAKES **INSULIN,** WHICH IS A HORMONE. INSULIN ALLOWS YOUR BODY TO USE SUGAR FROM THE FOOD YOU EAT TO GIVE YOU HEAT AND ENERGY.
WHEN THE PANCREAS DOESN'T MAKE **ENOUGH** INSULIN TO DO THE JOB, THE GLUCOSE FROM THE SUGARS BUILDS UP IN YOUR BLOOD AND MAKES YOU SICK.

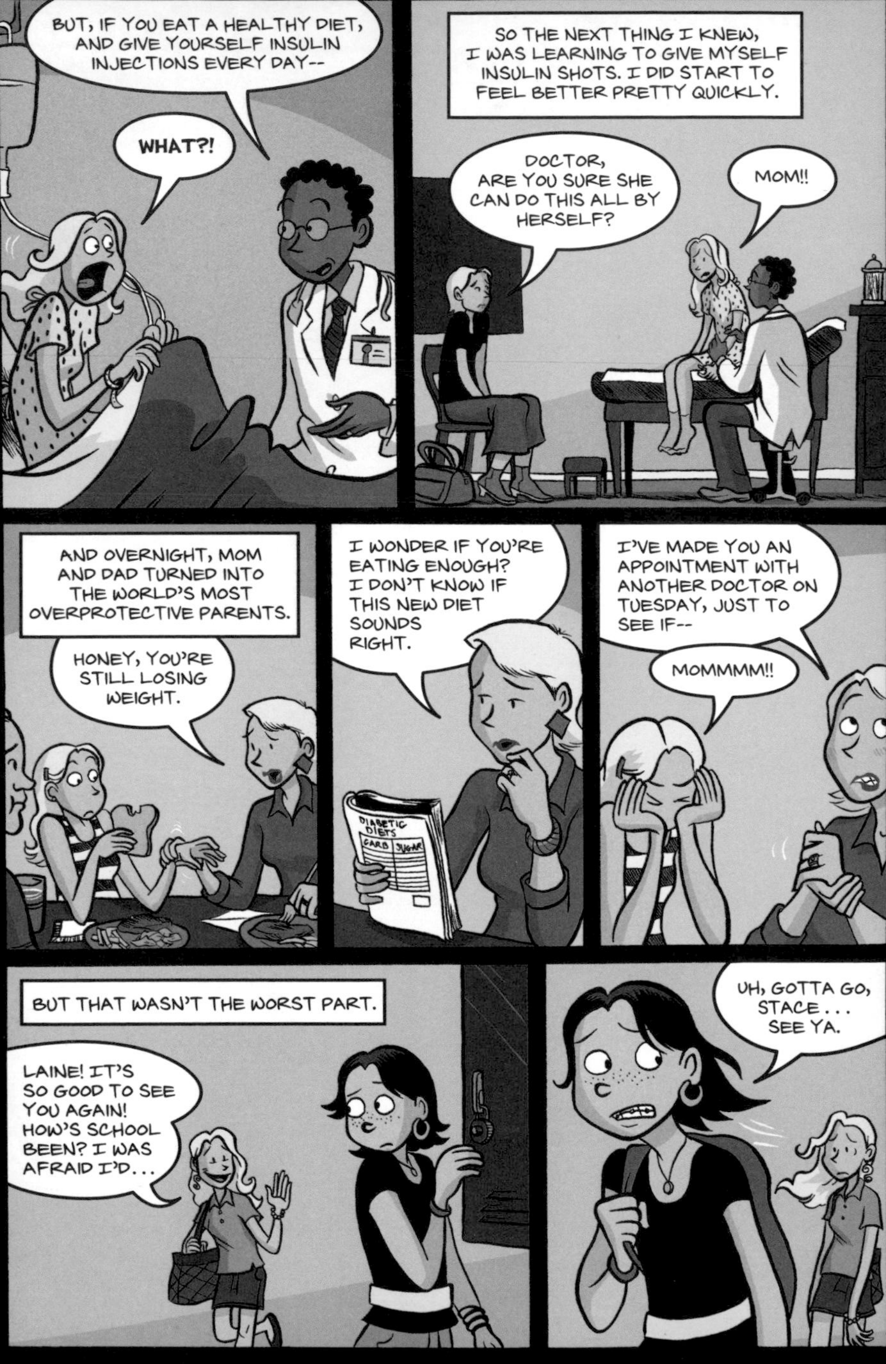
BUT, IF YOU EAT A HEALTHY DIET, AND GIVE YOURSELF INSULIN INJECTIONS EVERY DAY--
WHAT?!
SO THE NEXT THING I KNEW, I WAS LEARNING TO GIVE MYSELF INSULIN SHOTS. I DID START TO FEEL BETTER PRETTY QUICKLY.
DOCTOR, ARE YOU SURE SHE CAN DO THIS ALL BY HERSELF?
MOM!!
AND OVERNIGHT, MOM AND DAD TURNED INTO THE WORLD'S MOST OVERPROTECTIVE PARENTS.
HONEY, YOU'RE STILL LOSING WEIGHT.
I WONDER IF YOU'RE EATING ENOUGH? I DON'T KNOW IF THIS NEW DIET SOUNDS RIGHT.
DIABETIC DIETS
CARB SUGAR
I'VE MADE YOU AN APPOINTMENT WITH ANOTHER DOCTOR ON TUESDAY, JUST TO SEE IF--
MOMMMM!!
BUT THAT WASN'T THE WORST PART.
LAINE! IT'S SO GOOD TO SEE YOU AGAIN! HOW'S SCHOOL BEEN? I WAS AFRAID I'D. . .
UH, GOTTA GO, STACE . . . SEE YA.

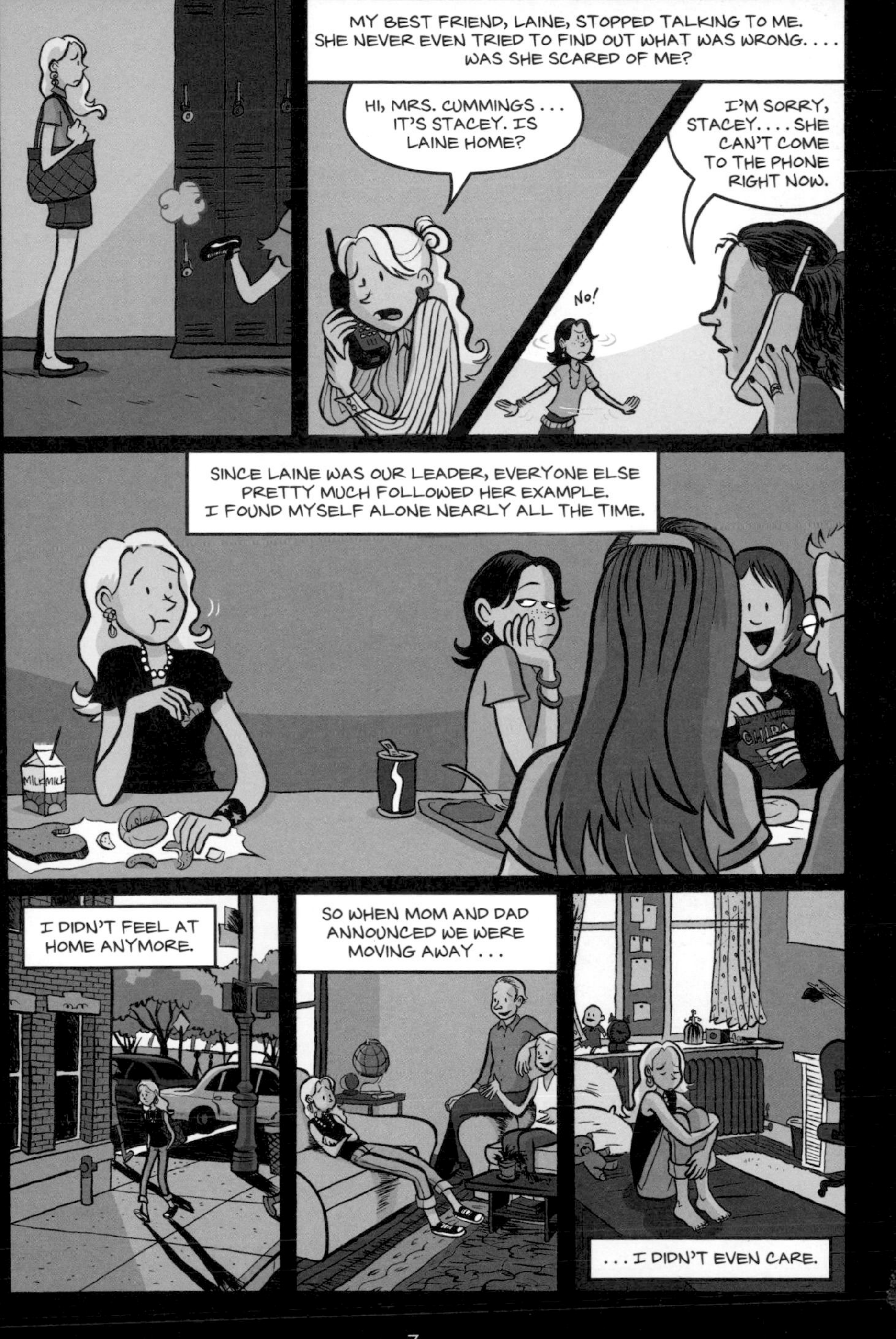

MY BEST FRIEND, LAINE, STOPPED TALKING TO ME. SHE NEVER EVEN TRIED TO FIND OUT WHAT WAS WRONG. . . . WAS SHE SCARED OF ME?
HI, MRS. CUMMINGS . . . IT'S STACEY. IS LAINE HOME?
I'M SORRY, STACEY. . . . SHE CAN'T COME TO THE PHONE RIGHT NOW.
NO!
SINCE LAINE WAS OUR LEADER, EVERYONE ELSE PRETTY MUCH FOLLOWED HER EXAMPLE. I FOUND MYSELF ALONE NEARLY ALL THE TIME.
MILK MILK
I DIDN'T FEEL AT HOME ANYMORE.
SO WHEN MOM AND DAD ANNOUNCED WE WERE MOVING AWAY . . .
. . . I DIDN'T EVEN CARE.

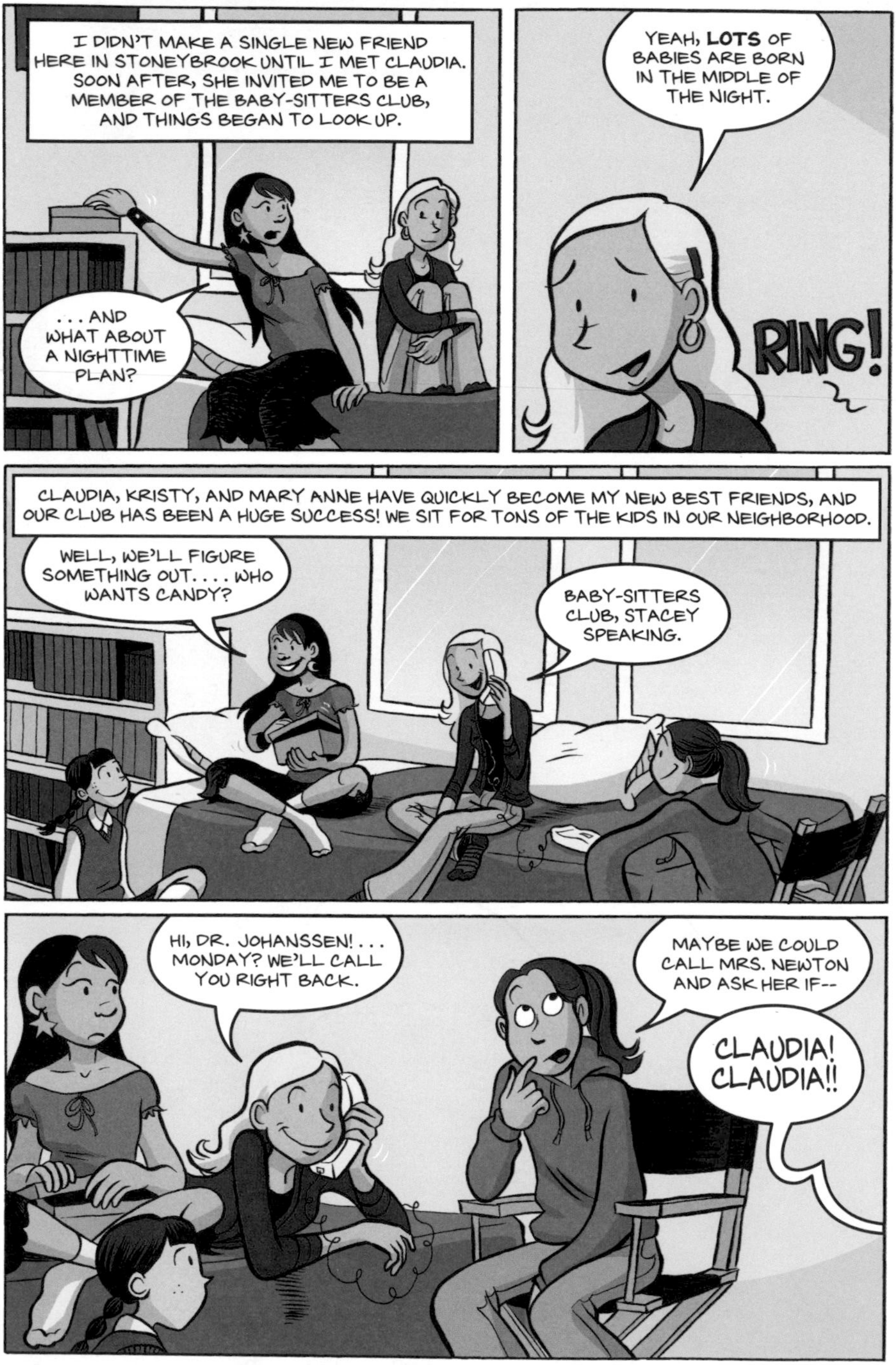
I DIDN'T MAKE A SINGLE NEW FRIEND HERE IN STONEYBROOK UNTIL I MET CLAUDIA. SOON AFTER, SHE INVITED ME TO BE A MEMBER OF THE BABY-SITTERS CLUB, AND THINGS BEGAN TO LOOK UP.
. . . AND WHAT ABOUT A NIGHTTIME PLAN?
YEAH, **LOTS** OF BABIES ARE BORN IN THE MIDDLE OF THE NIGHT.
RING!
CLAUDIA, KRISTY, AND MARY ANNE HAVE QUICKLY BECOME MY NEW BEST FRIENDS, AND OUR CLUB HAS BEEN A HUGE SUCCESS! WE SIT FOR TONS OF THE KIDS IN OUR NEIGHBORHOOD.
WELL, WE'LL FIGURE SOMETHING OUT. . . . WHO WANTS CANDY?
BABY-SITTERS CLUB, STACEY SPEAKING.
HI, DR. JOHANSSEN! . . . MONDAY? WE'LL CALL YOU RIGHT BACK.
MAYBE WE COULD CALL MRS. NEWTON AND ASK HER IF--
CLAUDIA! CLAUDIA!!

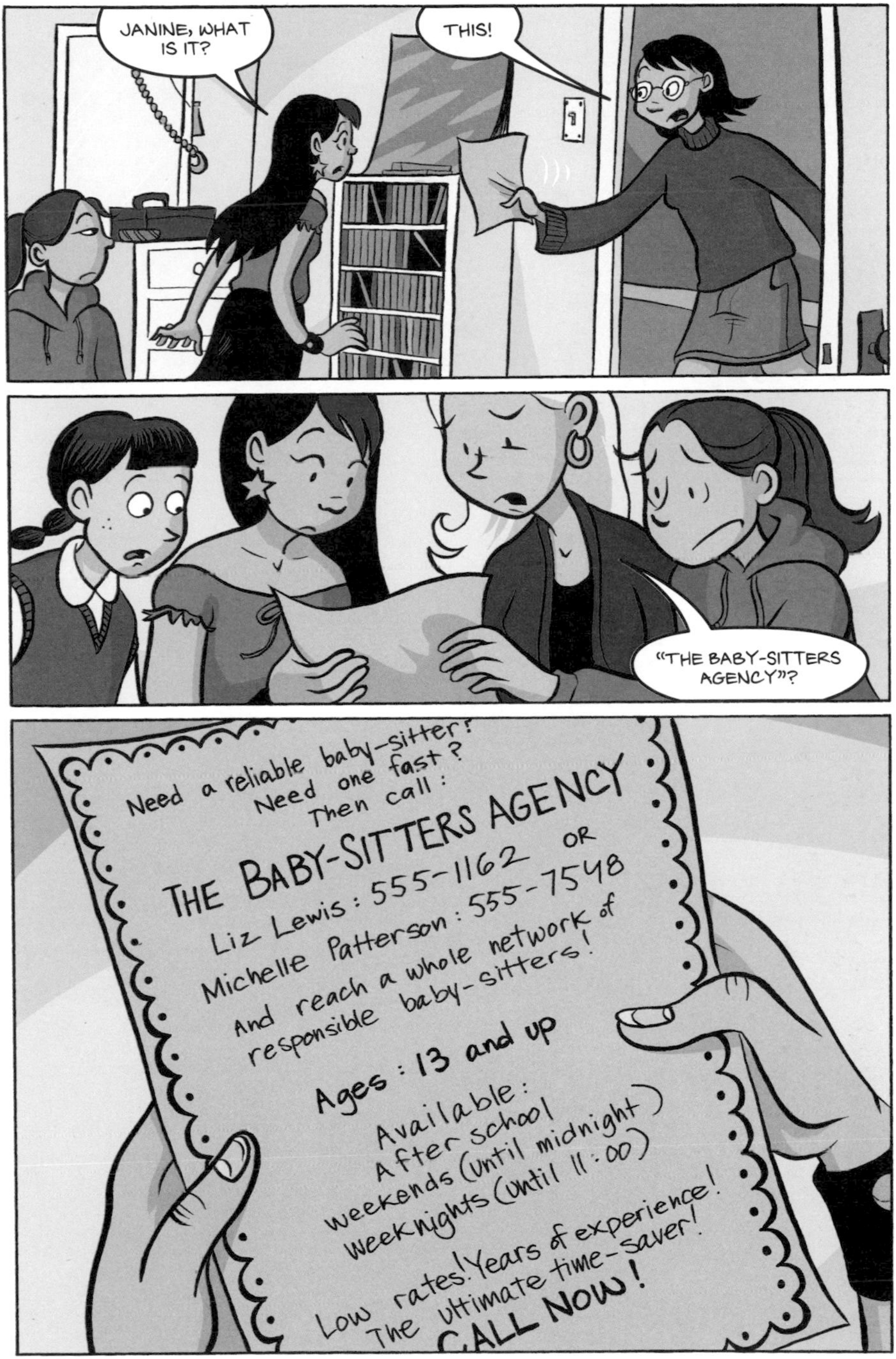
JANINE, WHAT IS IT?
THIS!
"THE BABY-SITTERS AGENCY"?
Need a reliable baby-sitter?
Need one fast?
Then call:
THE BABY-SITTERS AGENCY
Liz Lewis: 555-1162 OR
Michelle Patterson: 555-7548
And reach a whole network of responsible baby-sitters!
Ages: 13 and up
Available:
After school
weekends (until midnight)
weeknights (until 11:00)
Low rates! Years of experience!
The ultimate time-saver!
CALL NOW!

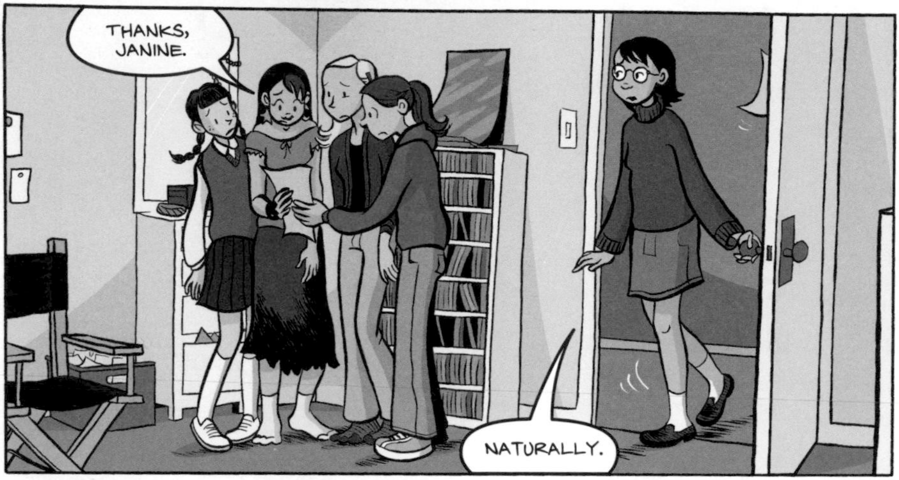
THANKS, JANINE.
NATURALLY.

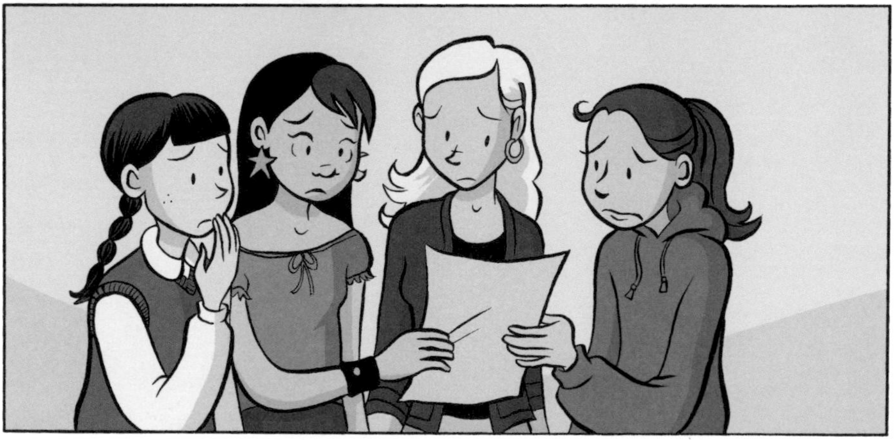

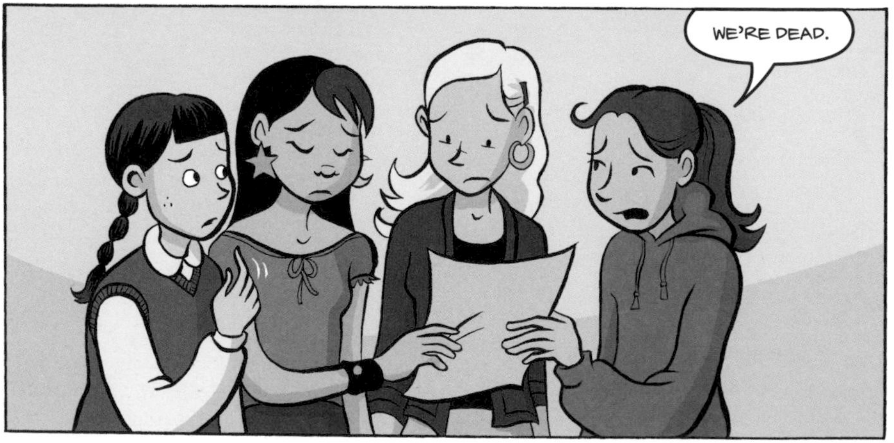
WE'RE DEAD.

CHAPTER 2

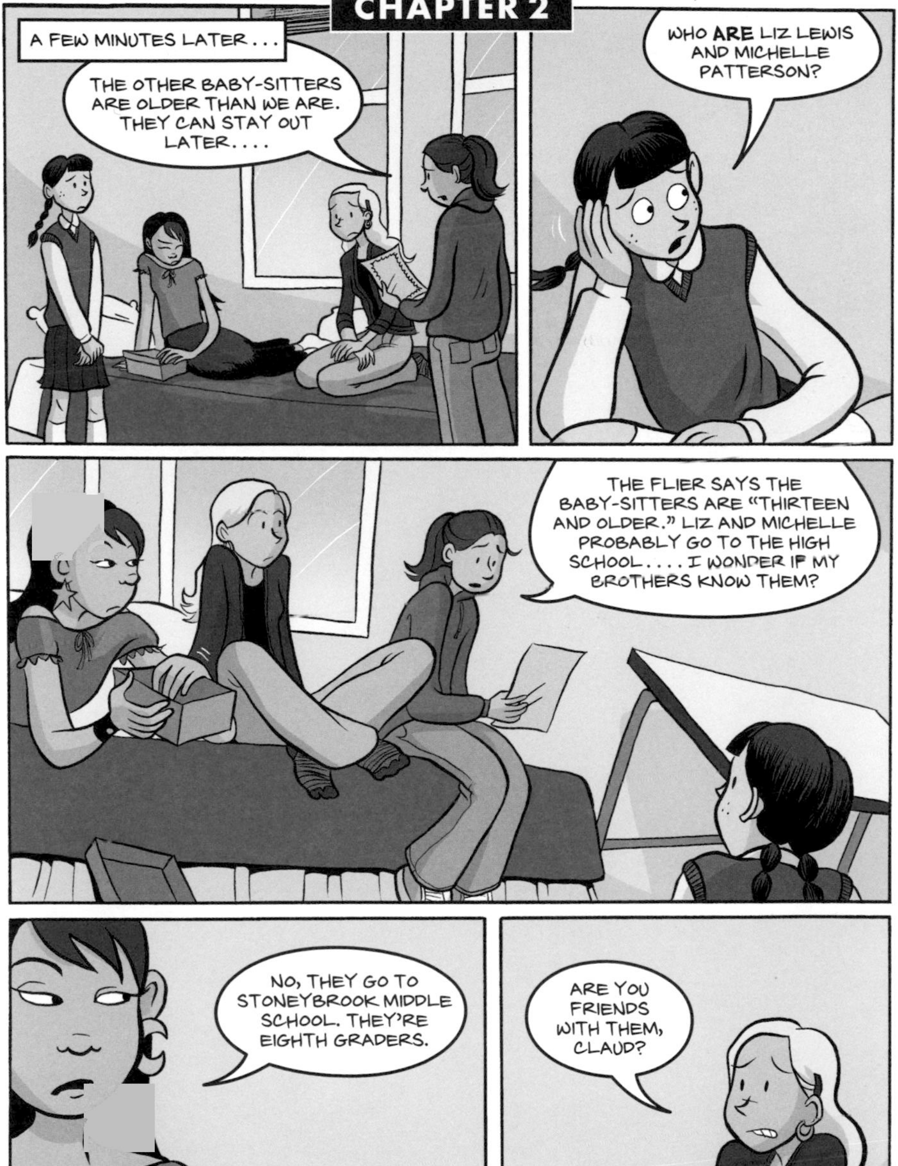
A FEW MINUTES LATER . . .
THE OTHER BABY-SITTERS ARE OLDER THAN WE ARE. THEY CAN STAY OUT LATER. . . .
WHO ARE LIZ LEWIS AND MICHELLE PATTERSON?
THE FLIER SAYS THE BABY-SITTERS ARE "THIRTEEN AND OLDER." LIZ AND MICHELLE PROBABLY GO TO THE HIGH SCHOOL . . . . I WONDER IF MY BROTHERS KNOW THEM?
NO, THEY GO TO STONEYBROOK MIDDLE SCHOOL. THEY'RE EIGHTH GRADERS.
RRRIP
ARE YOU FRIENDS WITH THEM, CLAUD?

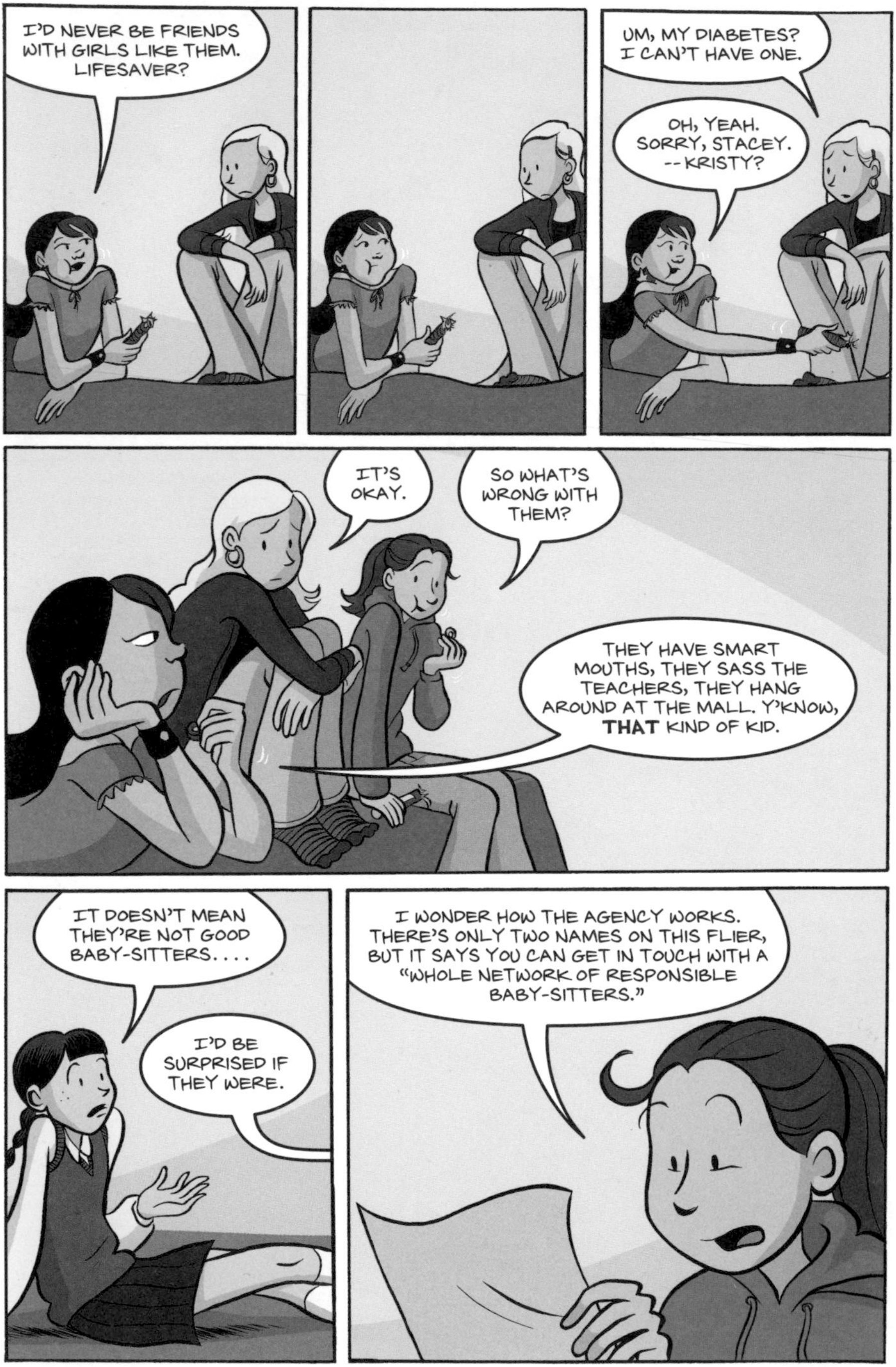
I'D NEVER BE FRIENDS WITH GIRLS LIKE THEM. LIFESAVER?
UM, MY DIABETES? I CAN'T HAVE ONE.
OH, YEAH. SORRY, STACEY. --KRISTY?
IT'S OKAY.
SO WHAT'S WRONG WITH THEM?
THEY HAVE SMART MOUTHS, THEY SASS THE TEACHERS, THEY HANG AROUND AT THE MALL. Y'KNOW, **THAT** KIND OF KID.
IT DOESN'T MEAN THEY'RE NOT GOOD BABY-SITTERS....
I'D BE SURPRISED IF THEY WERE.
I WONDER HOW THE AGENCY WORKS. THERE'S ONLY TWO NAMES ON THIS FLIER, BUT IT SAYS YOU CAN GET IN TOUCH WITH A "WHOLE NETWORK OF RESPONSIBLE BABY-SITTERS."

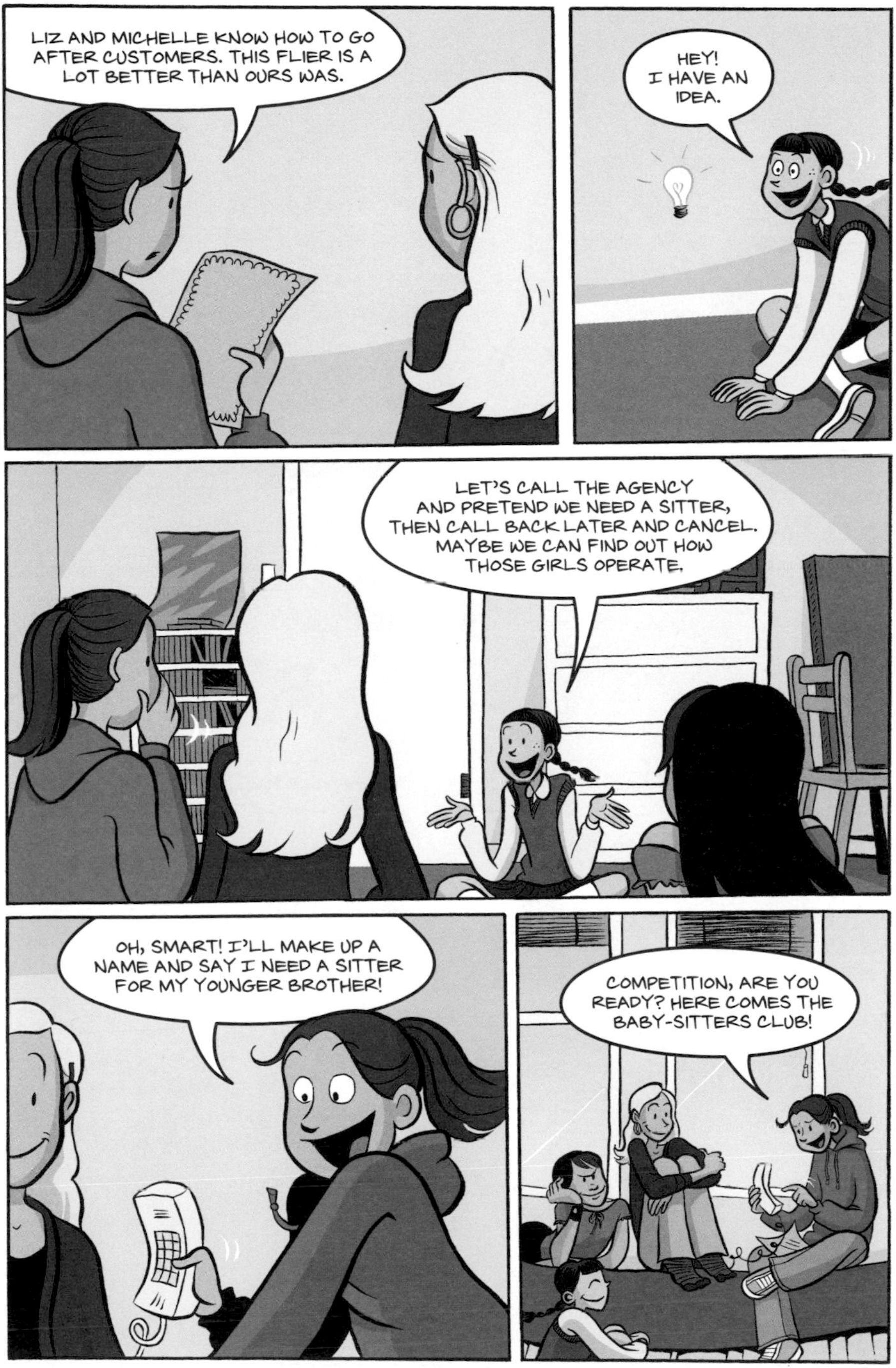
LIZ AND MICHELLE KNOW HOW TO GO AFTER CUSTOMERS. THIS FLIER IS A LOT BETTER THAN OURS WAS.
HEY! I HAVE AN IDEA.
LET'S CALL THE AGENCY AND PRETEND WE NEED A SITTER, THEN CALL BACK LATER AND CANCEL. MAYBE WE CAN FIND OUT HOW THOSE GIRLS OPERATE.
OH, SMART! I'LL MAKE UP A NAME AND SAY I NEED A SITTER FOR MY YOUNGER BROTHER!
COMPETITION, ARE YOU READY? HERE COMES THE BABY-SITTERS CLUB!

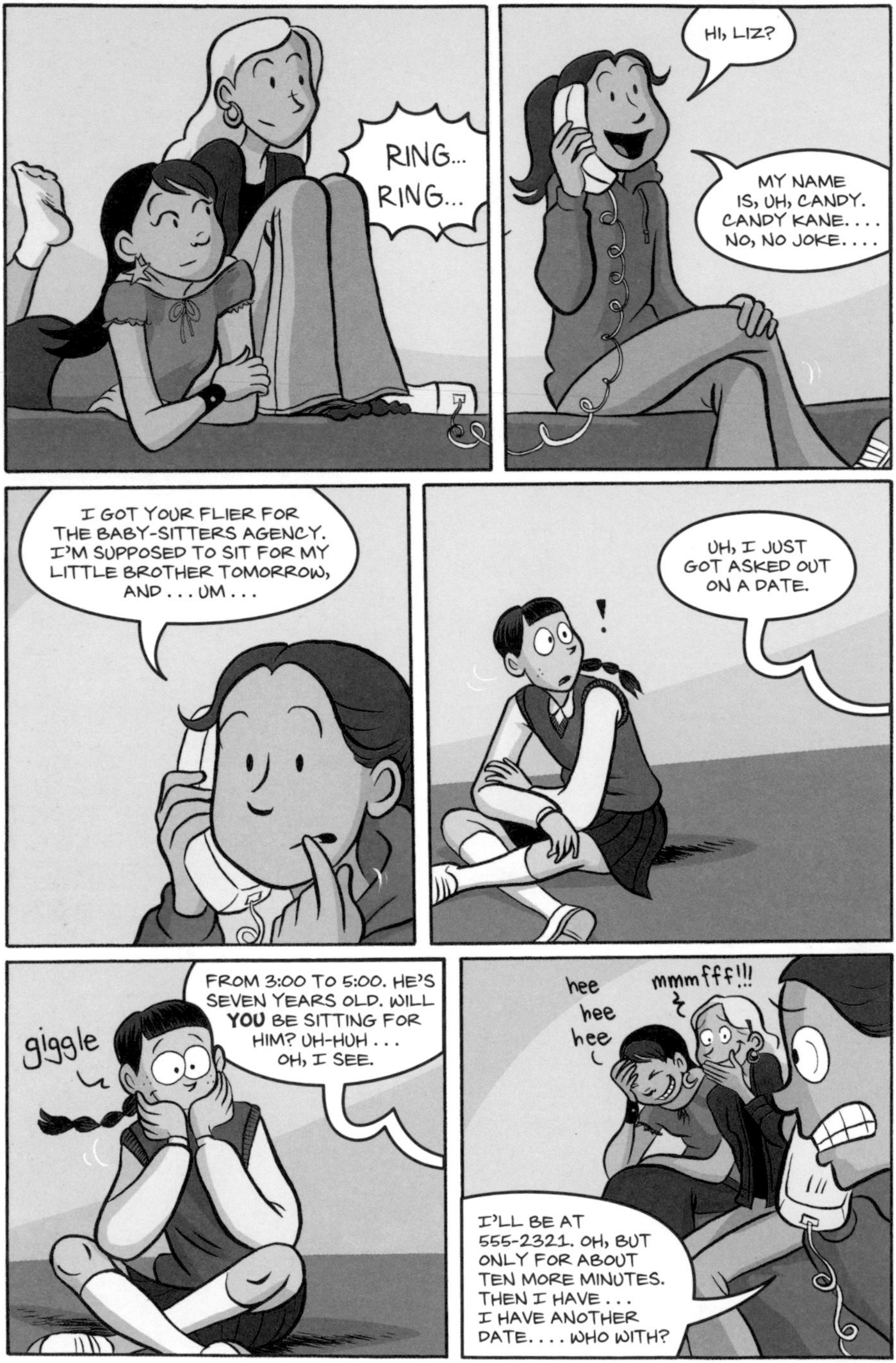
RING... RING...
HI, LIZ?
MY NAME IS, UH, CANDY. CANDY KANE. . . . NO, NO JOKE. . . .
I GOT YOUR FLIER FOR THE BABY-SITTERS AGENCY. I'M SUPPOSED TO SIT FOR MY LITTLE BROTHER TOMORROW, AND . . . UM . . .
!
UH, I JUST GOT ASKED OUT ON A DATE.
giggle
FROM 3:00 TO 5:00. HE'S SEVEN YEARS OLD. WILL **YOU** BE SITTING FOR HIM? UH-HUH . . . OH, I SEE.
hee hee hee
mmmfff!!!
I'LL BE AT 555-2321. OH, BUT ONLY FOR ABOUT TEN MORE MINUTES. THEN I HAVE . . . I HAVE ANOTHER DATE. . . . WHO WITH?

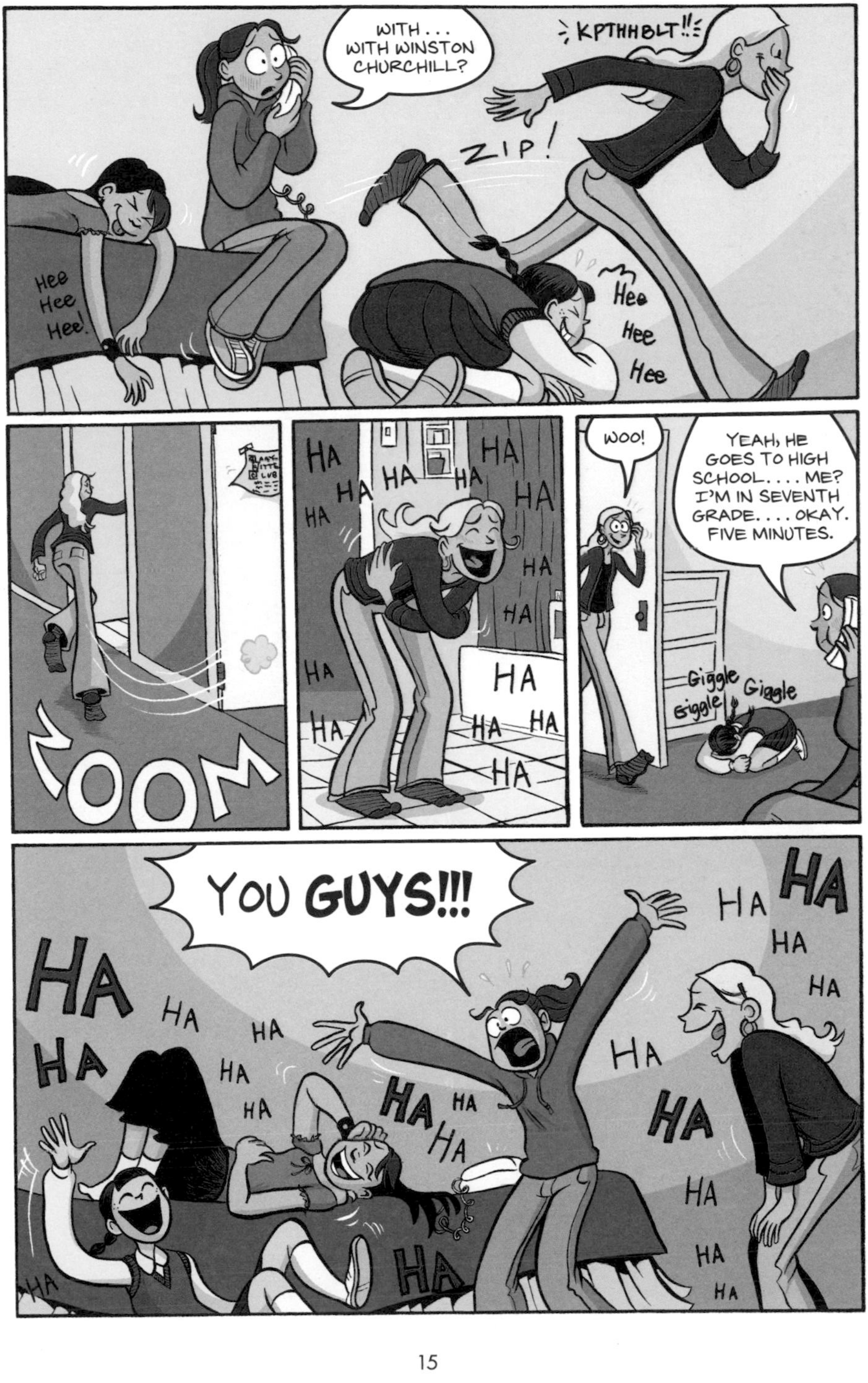
WITH... WITH WINSTON CHURCHILL?
KPTHHBLT!!
ZIP!
Hee Hee Hee!
Hee Hee Hee
ZOOM
HA HA HA HA HA HA HA HA HA HA HA
HA HA HA HA
WOO!
YEAH, HE GOES TO HIGH SCHOOL.... ME? I'M IN SEVENTH GRADE.... OKAY. FIVE MINUTES.
Giggle Giggle Giggle
YOU GUYS!!!
HA HA HA HA HA HA HA HA HA HA HA HA HA HA HA HA HA HA HA HA HA

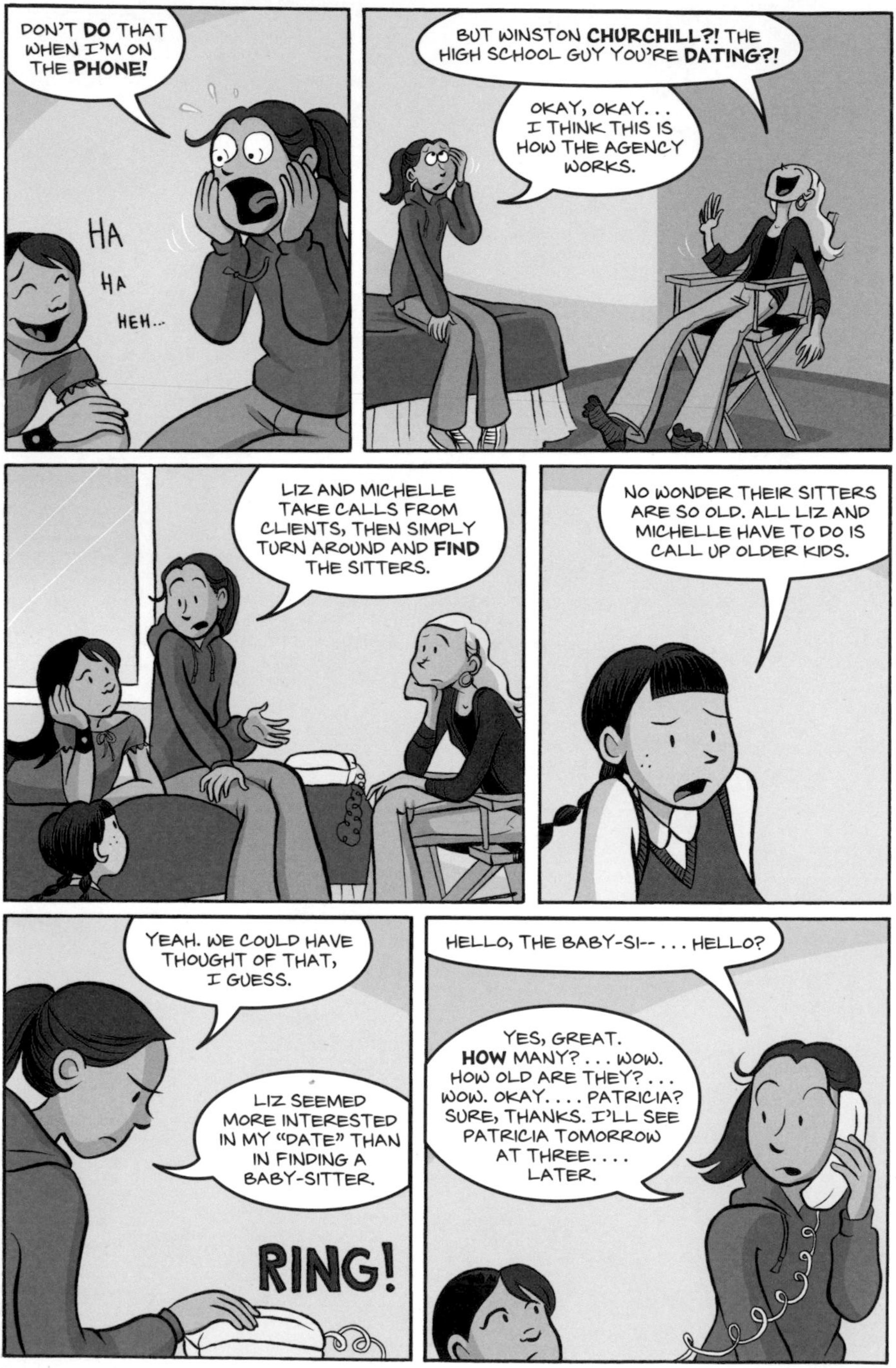
DON'T DO THAT WHEN I'M ON THE PHONE!
HA
HA
HEH...
BUT WINSTON CHURCHILL?! THE HIGH SCHOOL GUY YOU'RE DATING?!
OKAY, OKAY... I THINK THIS IS HOW THE AGENCY WORKS.
LIZ AND MICHELLE TAKE CALLS FROM CLIENTS, THEN SIMPLY TURN AROUND AND FIND THE SITTERS.
NO WONDER THEIR SITTERS ARE SO OLD. ALL LIZ AND MICHELLE HAVE TO DO IS CALL UP OLDER KIDS.
YEAH. WE COULD HAVE THOUGHT OF THAT, I GUESS.
LIZ SEEMED MORE INTERESTED IN MY "DATE" THAN IN FINDING A BABY-SITTER.
RING!
HELLO, THE BABY-SI-- . . . HELLO?
YES, GREAT. HOW MANY? . . . WOW. HOW OLD ARE THEY? . . . WOW. OKAY. . . . PATRICIA? SURE, THANKS. I'LL SEE PATRICIA TOMORROW AT THREE. . . . LATER.

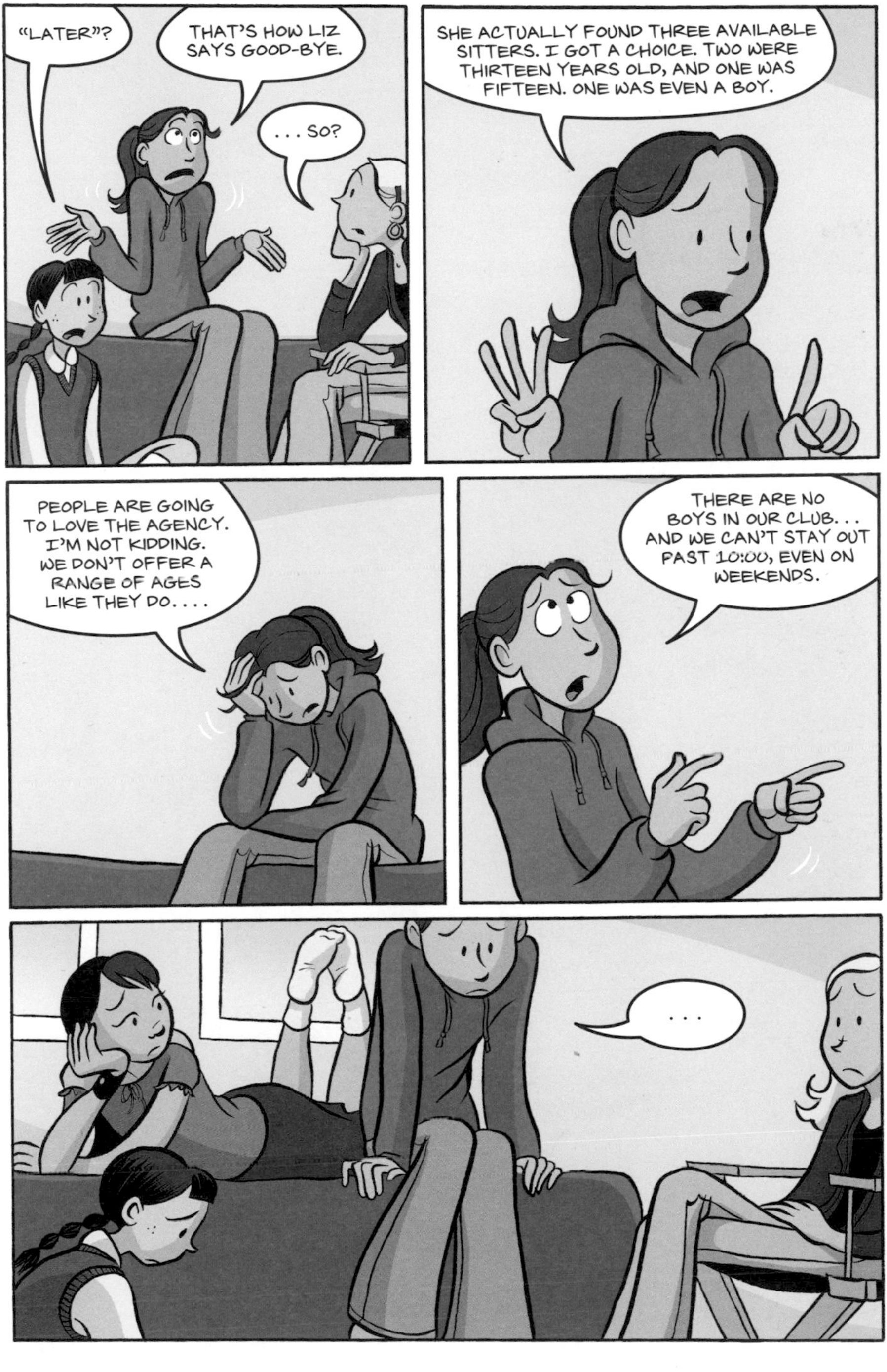
"LATER"?
THAT'S HOW LIZ SAYS GOOD-BYE.
. . . SO?
SHE ACTUALLY FOUND THREE AVAILABLE SITTERS. I GOT A CHOICE. TWO WERE THIRTEEN YEARS OLD, AND ONE WAS FIFTEEN. ONE WAS EVEN A BOY.
PEOPLE ARE GOING TO LOVE THE AGENCY. I'M NOT KIDDING. WE DON'T OFFER A RANGE OF AGES LIKE THEY DO. . . .
THERE ARE NO BOYS IN OUR CLUB. . . AND WE CAN'T STAY OUT PAST 10:00, EVEN ON WEEKENDS.
. . .

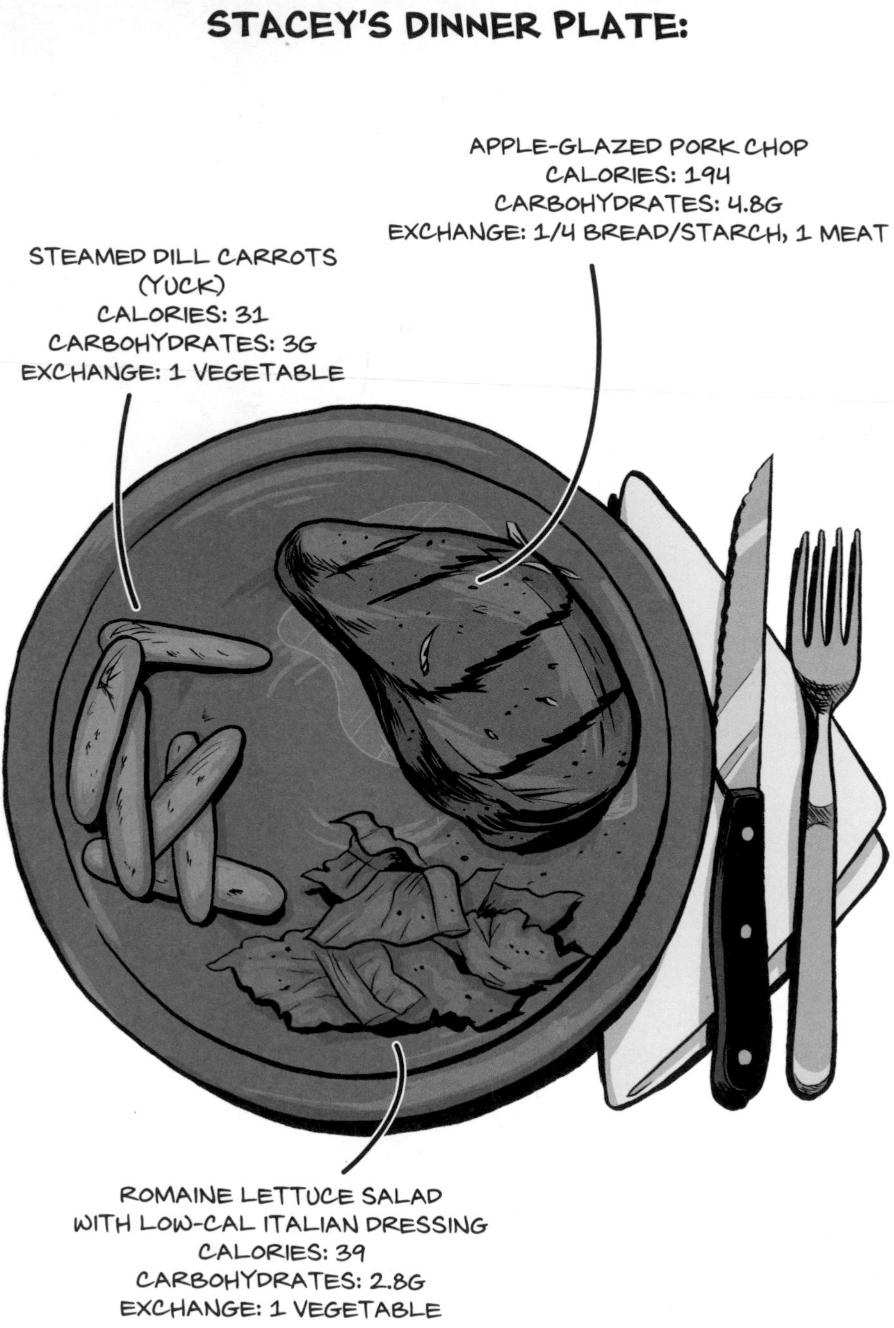
STACEY'S DINNER PLATE:
APPLE-GLAZED PORK CHOP
CALORIES: 194
CARBOHYDRATES: 4.8G
EXCHANGE: 1/4 BREAD/STARCH, 1 MEAT
STEAMED DILL CARROTS
(YUCK)
CALORIES: 31
CARBOHYDRATES: 3G
EXCHANGE: 1 VEGETABLE
ROMAINE LETTUCE SALAD
WITH LOW-CAL ITALIAN DRESSING
CALORIES: 39
CARBOHYDRATES: 2.8G
EXCHANGE: 1 VEGETABLE

CHAPTER 3

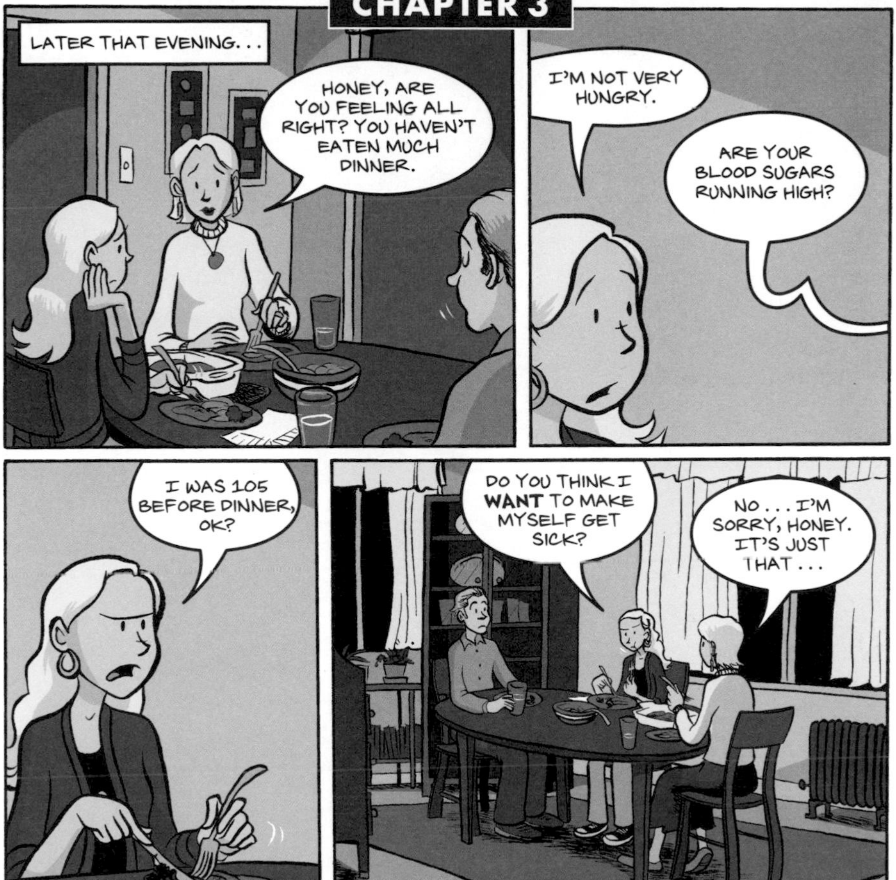

LATER THAT EVENING...
HONEY, ARE YOU FEELING ALL RIGHT? YOU HAVEN'T EATEN MUCH DINNER.
I'M NOT VERY HUNGRY.
ARE YOUR BLOOD SUGARS RUNNING HIGH?
I WAS 105 BEFORE DINNER, OK?
DO YOU THINK I **WANT** TO MAKE MYSELF GET SICK?
NO... I'M SORRY, HONEY. IT'S JUST THAT...
YOU'VE LOST THREE POUNDS THIS MONTH, AND... ARE YOU **SURE** YOU'RE FEELING ALL RIGHT?
YES. MAYBE I'M MORE ACTIVE NOW THAT I HAVE SOME FRIENDS HERE. MAYBE I NEED TO EAT **MORE.**
BUT YOU JUST SAID YOU WEREN'T HUNGRY. I'LL CALL THE DOCTOR ON MONDAY.
JUST IN CASE.

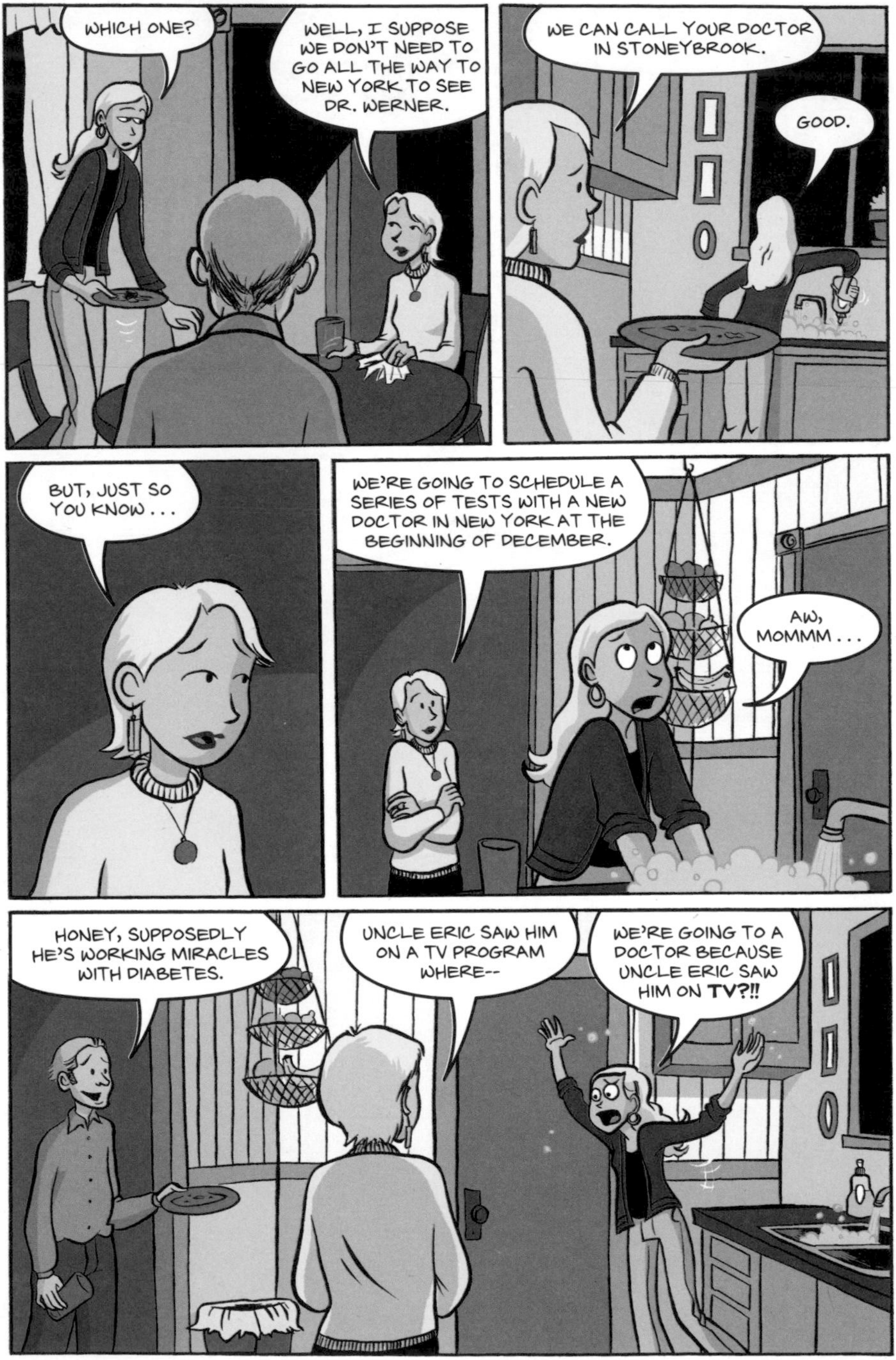
WHICH ONE?
WELL, I SUPPOSE WE DON'T NEED TO GO ALL THE WAY TO NEW YORK TO SEE DR. WERNER.
WE CAN CALL YOUR DOCTOR IN STONEYBROOK.
GOOD.
BUT, JUST SO YOU KNOW . . .
WE'RE GOING TO SCHEDULE A SERIES OF TESTS WITH A NEW DOCTOR IN NEW YORK AT THE BEGINNING OF DECEMBER.
AW, MOMMM . . .
HONEY, SUPPOSEDLY HE'S WORKING MIRACLES WITH DIABETES.
UNCLE ERIC SAW HIM ON A TV PROGRAM WHERE--
WE'RE GOING TO A DOCTOR BECAUSE UNCLE ERIC SAW HIM ON **TV?!!**

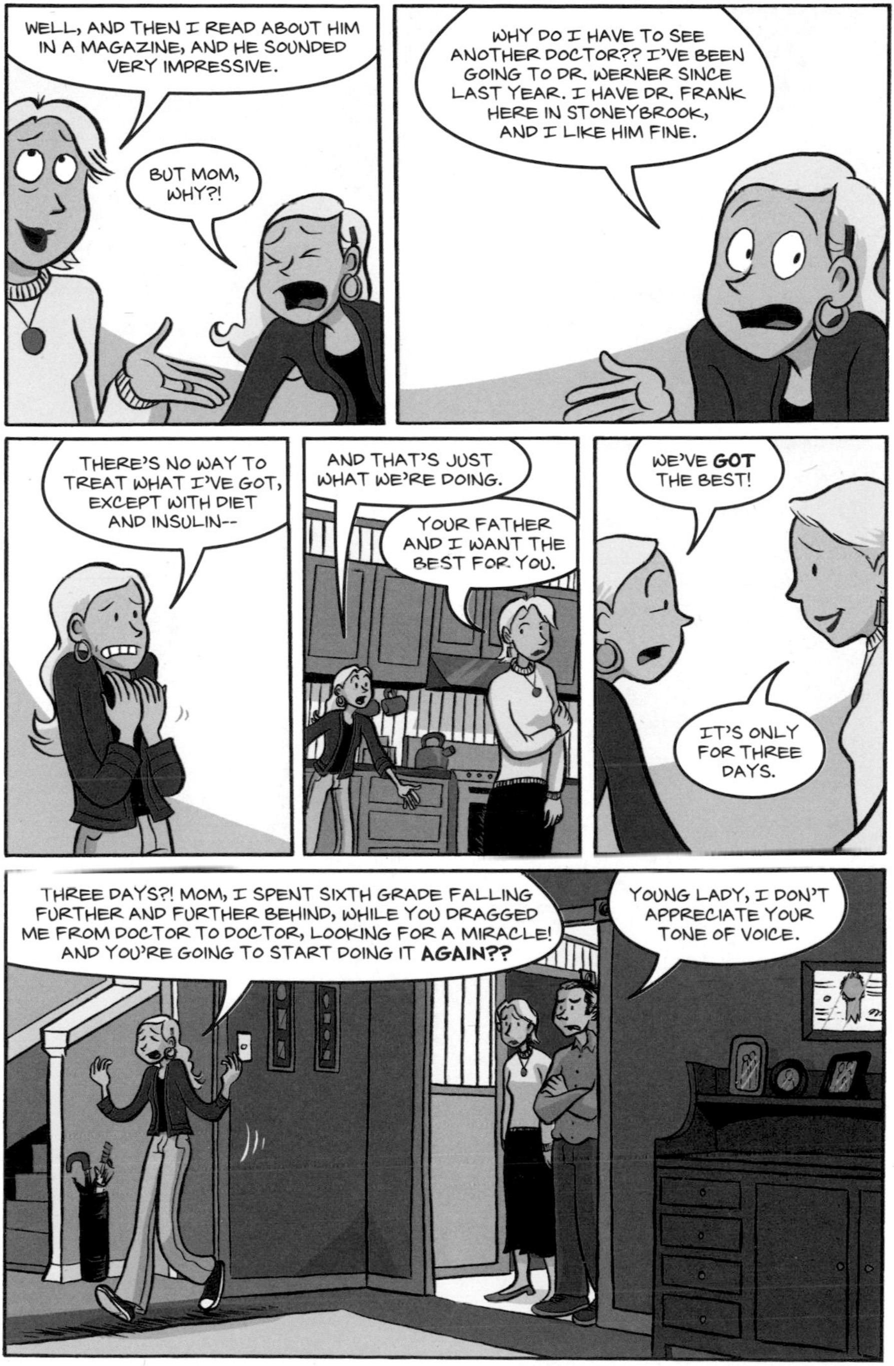
WELL, AND THEN I READ ABOUT HIM IN A MAGAZINE, AND HE SOUNDED VERY IMPRESSIVE.
BUT MOM, WHY?!
WHY DO I HAVE TO SEE ANOTHER DOCTOR?? I'VE BEEN GOING TO DR. WERNER SINCE LAST YEAR. I HAVE DR. FRANK HERE IN STONEYBROOK, AND I LIKE HIM FINE.
THERE'S NO WAY TO TREAT WHAT I'VE GOT, EXCEPT WITH DIET AND INSULIN--
AND THAT'S JUST WHAT WE'RE DOING.
YOUR FATHER AND I WANT THE BEST FOR YOU.
WE'VE **GOT** THE BEST!
IT'S ONLY FOR THREE DAYS.
THREE DAYS?! MOM, I SPENT SIXTH GRADE FALLING FURTHER AND FURTHER BEHIND, WHILE YOU DRAGGED ME FROM DOCTOR TO DOCTOR, LOOKING FOR A MIRACLE! AND YOU'RE GOING TO START DOING IT **AGAIN??**
YOUNG LADY, I DON'T APPRECIATE YOUR TONE OF VOICE.

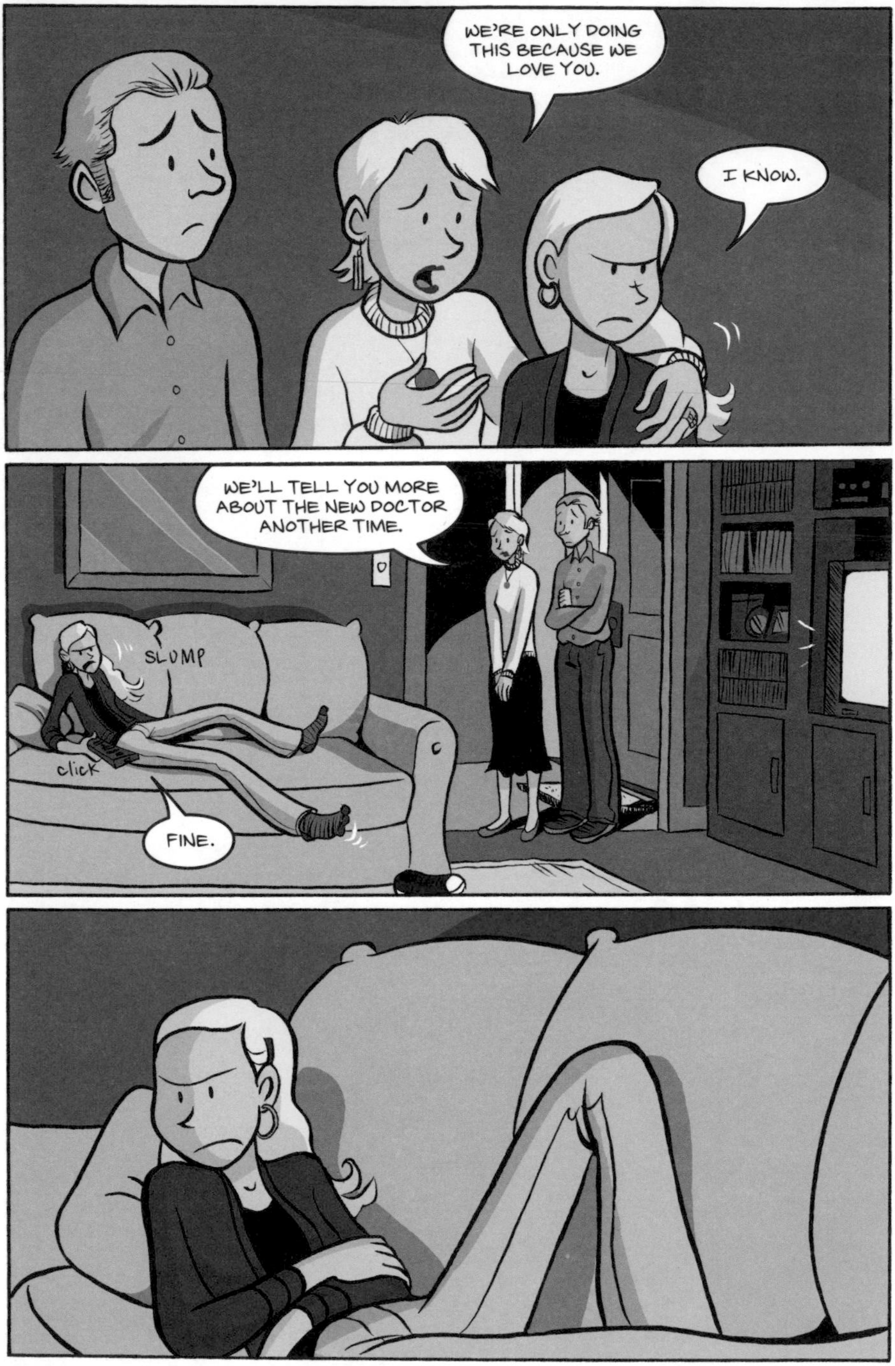
WE'RE ONLY DOING THIS BECAUSE WE LOVE YOU.
I KNOW.
WE'LL TELL YOU MORE ABOUT THE NEW DOCTOR ANOTHER TIME.
SLUMP
click
FINE.

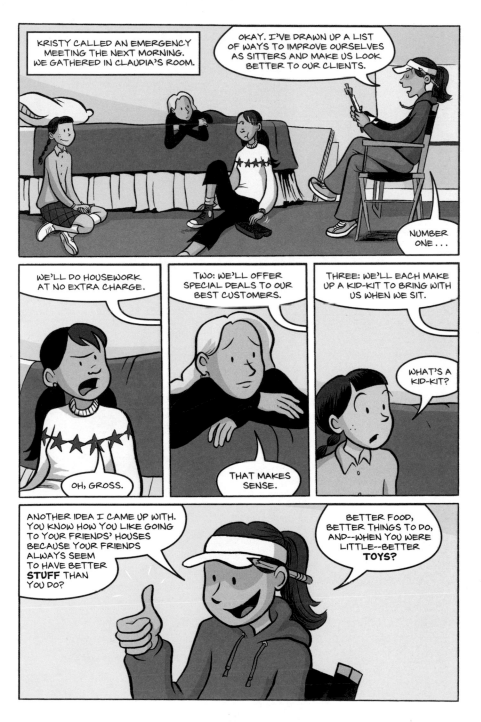

KRISTY CALLED AN EMERGENCY MEETING THE NEXT MORNING. WE GATHERED IN CLAUDIA'S ROOM.

OKAY. I'VE DRAWN UP A LIST OF WAYS TO IMPROVE OURSELVES AS SITTERS AND MAKE US LOOK BETTER TO OUR CLIENTS.

NUMBER ONE...

WE'LL DO HOUSEWORK AT NO EXTRA CHARGE.

OH, GROSS.

TWO: WE'LL OFFER SPECIAL DEALS TO OUR BEST CUSTOMERS.

THAT MAKES SENSE.

THREE: WE'LL EACH MAKE UP A KID-KIT TO BRING WITH US WHEN WE SIT.

WHAT'S A KID-KIT?

ANOTHER IDEA I CAME UP WITH. YOU KNOW HOW YOU LIKE GOING TO YOUR FRIENDS' HOUSES BECAUSE YOUR FRIENDS ALWAYS SEEM TO HAVE BETTER **STUFF** THAN YOU DO?

BETTER FOOD, BETTER THINGS TO DO, AND--WHEN YOU WERE LITTLE--BETTER **TOYS?**

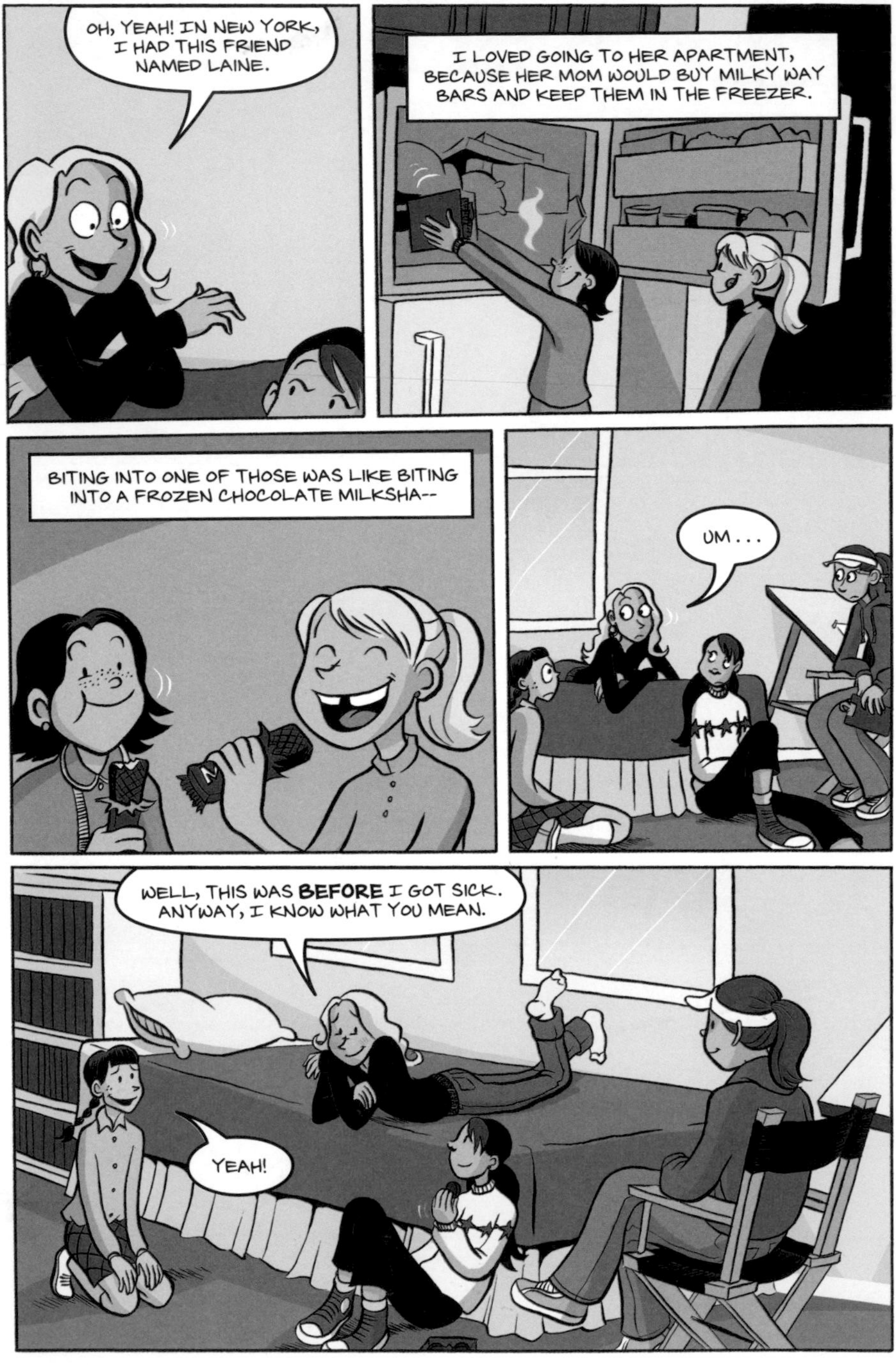
OH, YEAH! IN NEW YORK, I HAD THIS FRIEND NAMED LAINE.
I LOVED GOING TO HER APARTMENT, BECAUSE HER MOM WOULD BUY MILKY WAY BARS AND KEEP THEM IN THE FREEZER.
BITING INTO ONE OF THOSE WAS LIKE BITING INTO A FROZEN CHOCOLATE MILKSHA--
UM . . .
WELL, THIS WAS **BEFORE** I GOT SICK. ANYWAY, I KNOW WHAT YOU MEAN.
YEAH!

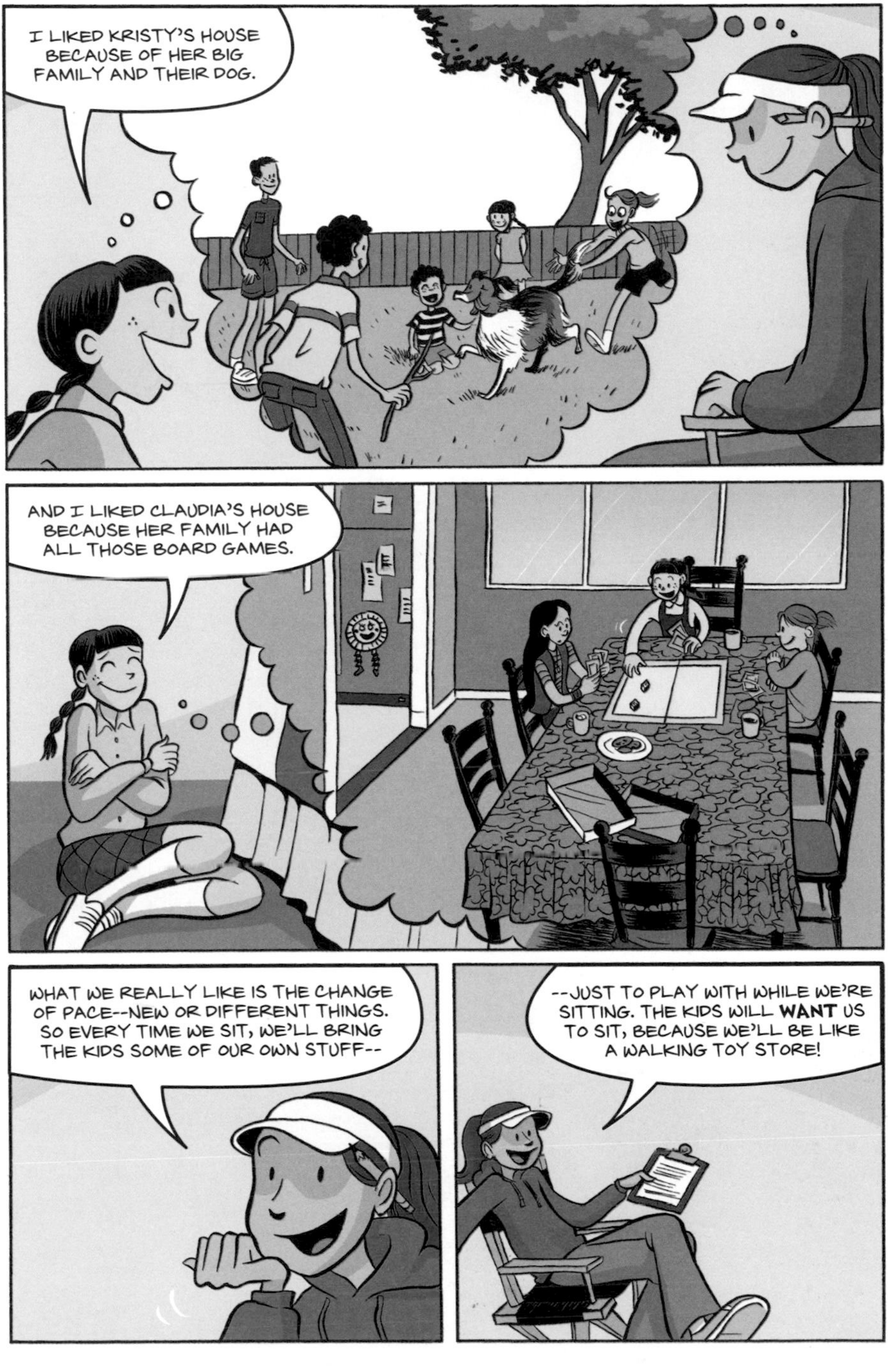
I LIKED KRISTY'S HOUSE BECAUSE OF HER BIG FAMILY AND THEIR DOG.
AND I LIKED CLAUDIA'S HOUSE BECAUSE HER FAMILY HAD ALL THOSE BOARD GAMES.
WHAT WE REALLY LIKE IS THE CHANGE OF PACE--NEW OR DIFFERENT THINGS. SO EVERY TIME WE SIT, WE'LL BRING THE KIDS SOME OF OUR OWN STUFF--
--JUST TO PLAY WITH WHILE WE'RE SITTING. THE KIDS WILL **WANT** US TO SIT, BECAUSE WE'LL BE LIKE A WALKING TOY STORE!

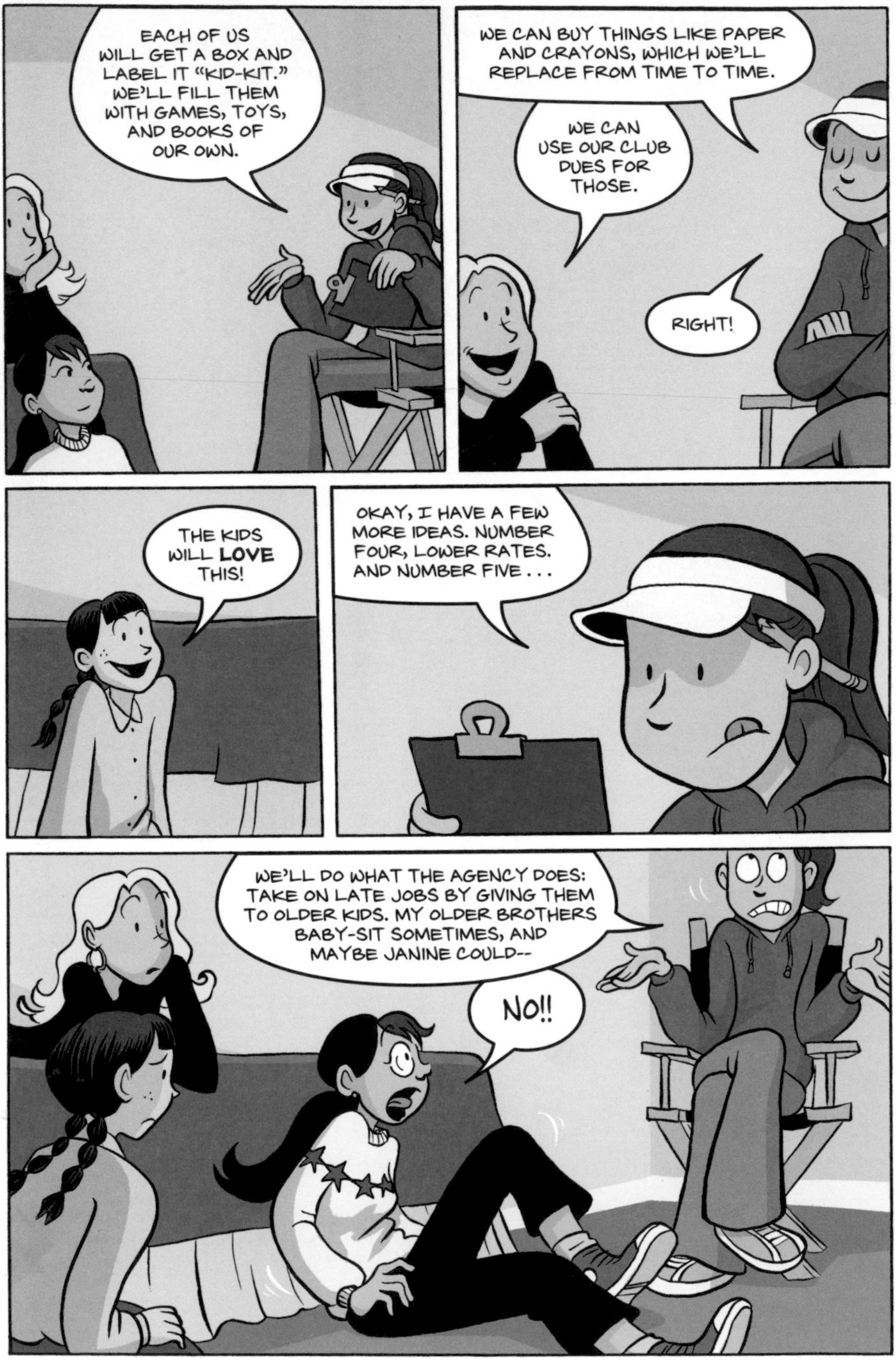
EACH OF US WILL GET A BOX AND LABEL IT "KID-KIT." WE'LL FILL THEM WITH GAMES, TOYS, AND BOOKS OF OUR OWN.
WE CAN BUY THINGS LIKE PAPER AND CRAYONS, WHICH WE'LL REPLACE FROM TIME TO TIME.
WE CAN USE OUR CLUB DUES FOR THOSE.
RIGHT!
THE KIDS WILL **LOVE** THIS!
OKAY, I HAVE A FEW MORE IDEAS. NUMBER FOUR, LOWER RATES. AND NUMBER FIVE . . .
WE'LL DO WHAT THE AGENCY DOES: TAKE ON LATE JOBS BY GIVING THEM TO OLDER KIDS. MY OLDER BROTHERS BABY-SIT SOMETIMES, AND MAYBE JANINE COULD--
NO!!

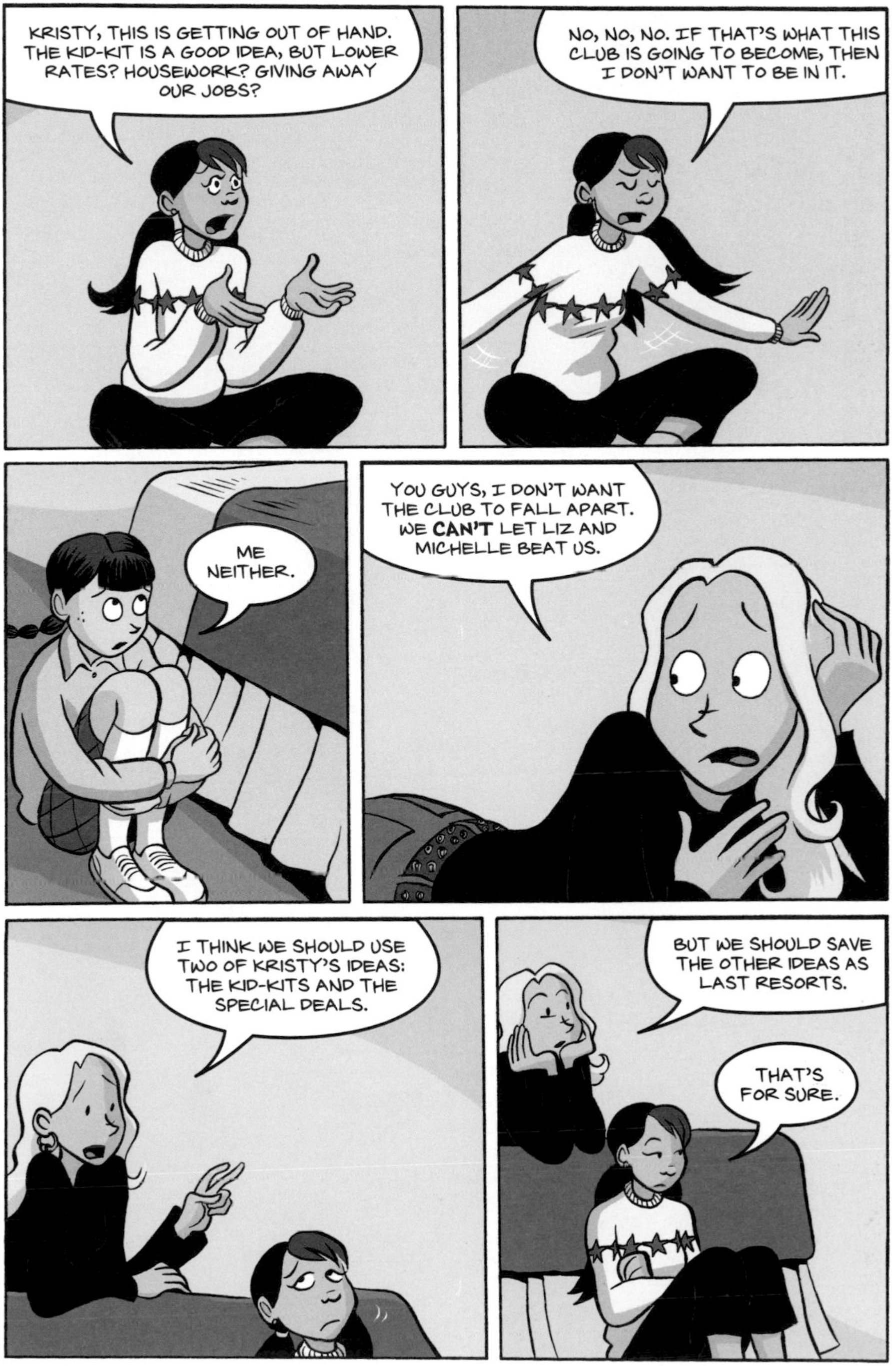
KRISTY, THIS IS GETTING OUT OF HAND. THE KID-KIT IS A GOOD IDEA, BUT LOWER RATES? HOUSEWORK? GIVING AWAY OUR JOBS?
NO, NO, NO. IF THAT'S WHAT THIS CLUB IS GOING TO BECOME, THEN I DON'T WANT TO BE IN IT.
ME NEITHER.
YOU GUYS, I DON'T WANT THE CLUB TO FALL APART. WE **CAN'T** LET LIZ AND MICHELLE BEAT US.
I THINK WE SHOULD USE TWO OF KRISTY'S IDEAS: THE KID-KITS AND THE SPECIAL DEALS.
BUT WE SHOULD SAVE THE OTHER IDEAS AS LAST RESORTS.
THAT'S FOR SURE.

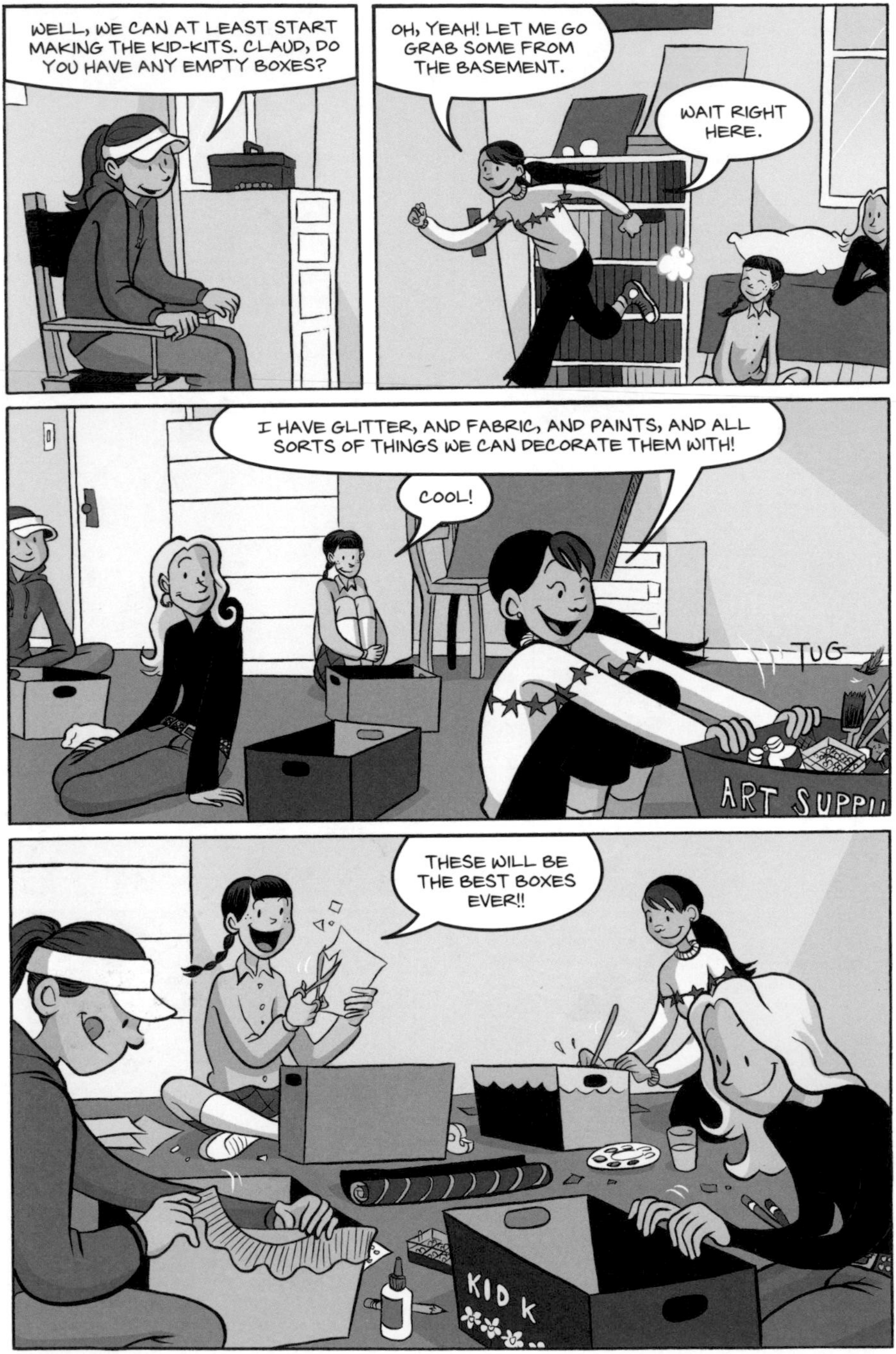
WELL, WE CAN AT LEAST START MAKING THE KID-KITS. CLAUD, DO YOU HAVE ANY EMPTY BOXES?
OH, YEAH! LET ME GO GRAB SOME FROM THE BASEMENT.
WAIT RIGHT HERE.
I HAVE GLITTER, AND FABRIC, AND PAINTS, AND ALL SORTS OF THINGS WE CAN DECORATE THEM WITH!
COOL!
TUG
ART SUPPLI
THESE WILL BE THE BEST BOXES EVER!!
KID K

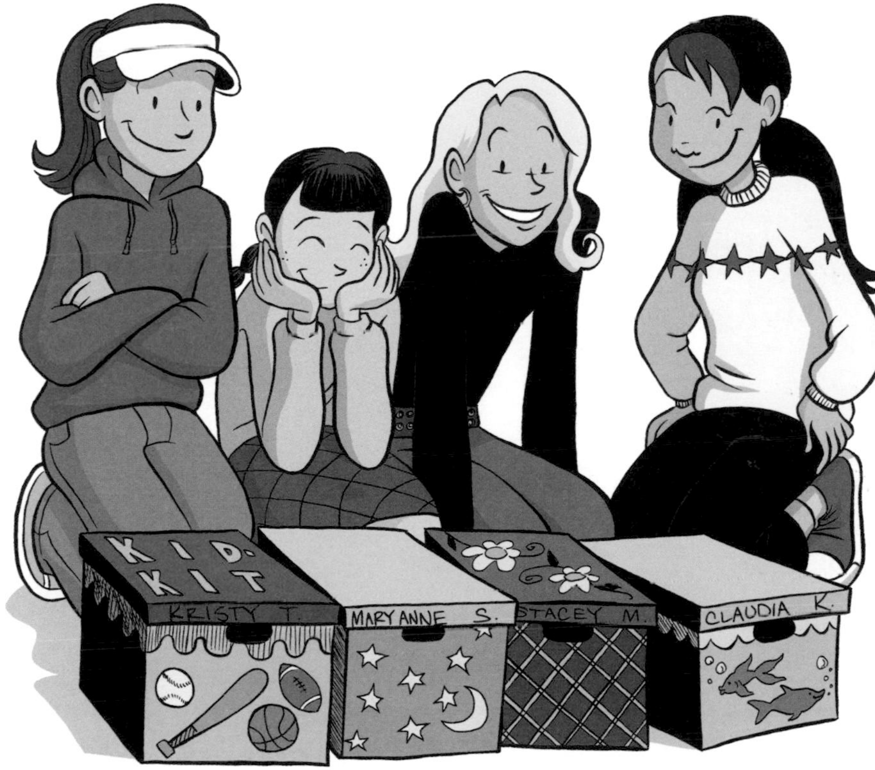

KID-KIT
KRISTY T.
MARY ANNE S.
STACEY M.
CLAUDIA K.

November 10

Monday I had a sitting job for Charlotte Johanssen. I love sitting for Charlotte, she's one of my very favorite kids. And her mother, Dr. Johanssen, is a Doctor at Stoneybrook Medical Center, so I like talking to her — she always asks me how I'm doing and how I feel about my treatments. Today was no different, except for what happened near the end of the afternoon . . .

Stacey

CHAPTER 4

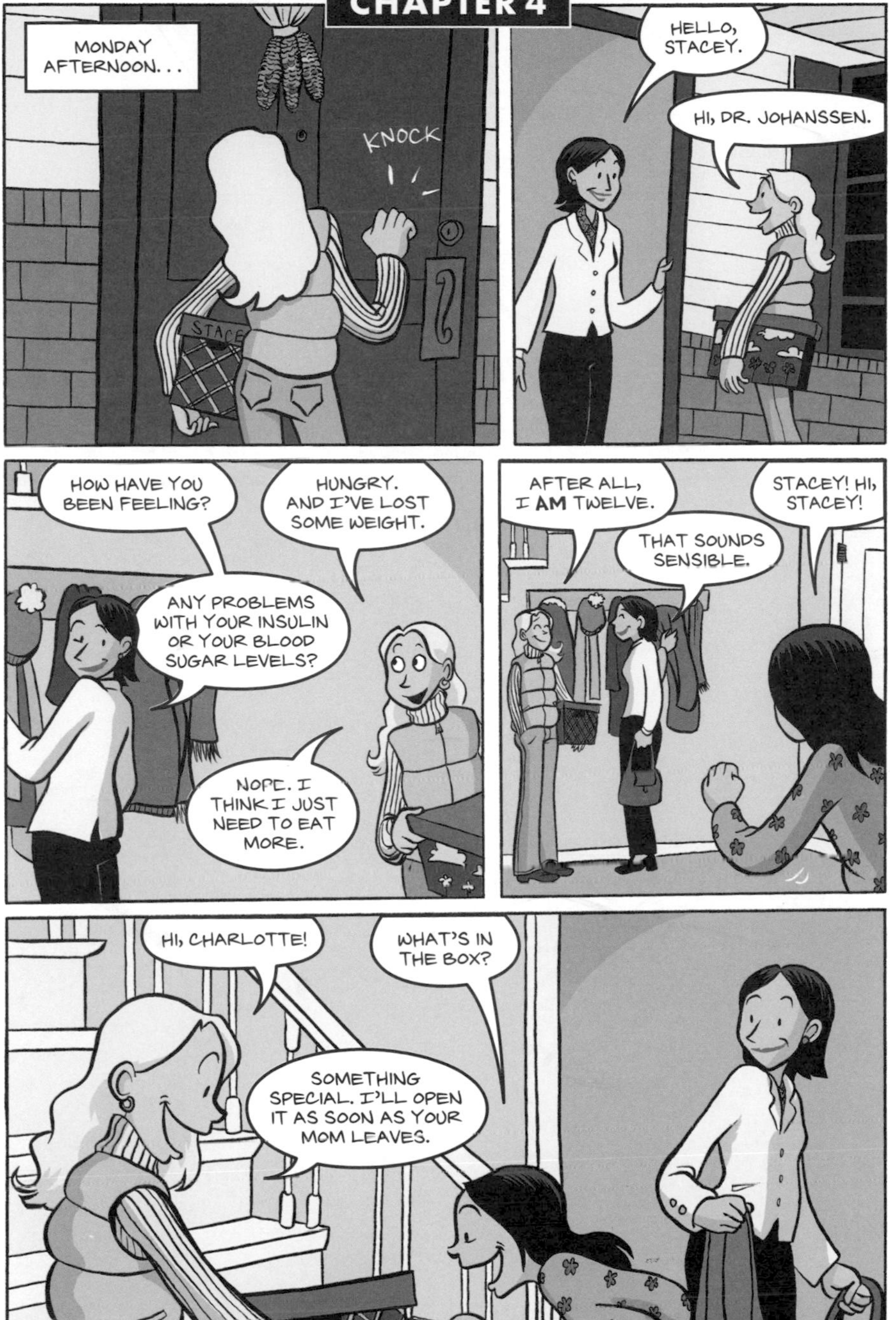
MONDAY AFTERNOON. . .
KNOCK
HELLO, STACEY.
HI, DR. JOHANSSEN.
HOW HAVE YOU BEEN FEELING?
HUNGRY. AND I'VE LOST SOME WEIGHT.
ANY PROBLEMS WITH YOUR INSULIN OR YOUR BLOOD SUGAR LEVELS?
NOPE. I THINK I JUST NEED TO EAT MORE.
AFTER ALL, I AM TWELVE.
THAT SOUNDS SENSIBLE.
STACEY! HI, STACEY!
HI, CHARLOTTE!
WHAT'S IN THE BOX?
SOMETHING SPECIAL. I'LL OPEN IT AS SOON AS YOUR MOM LEAVES.

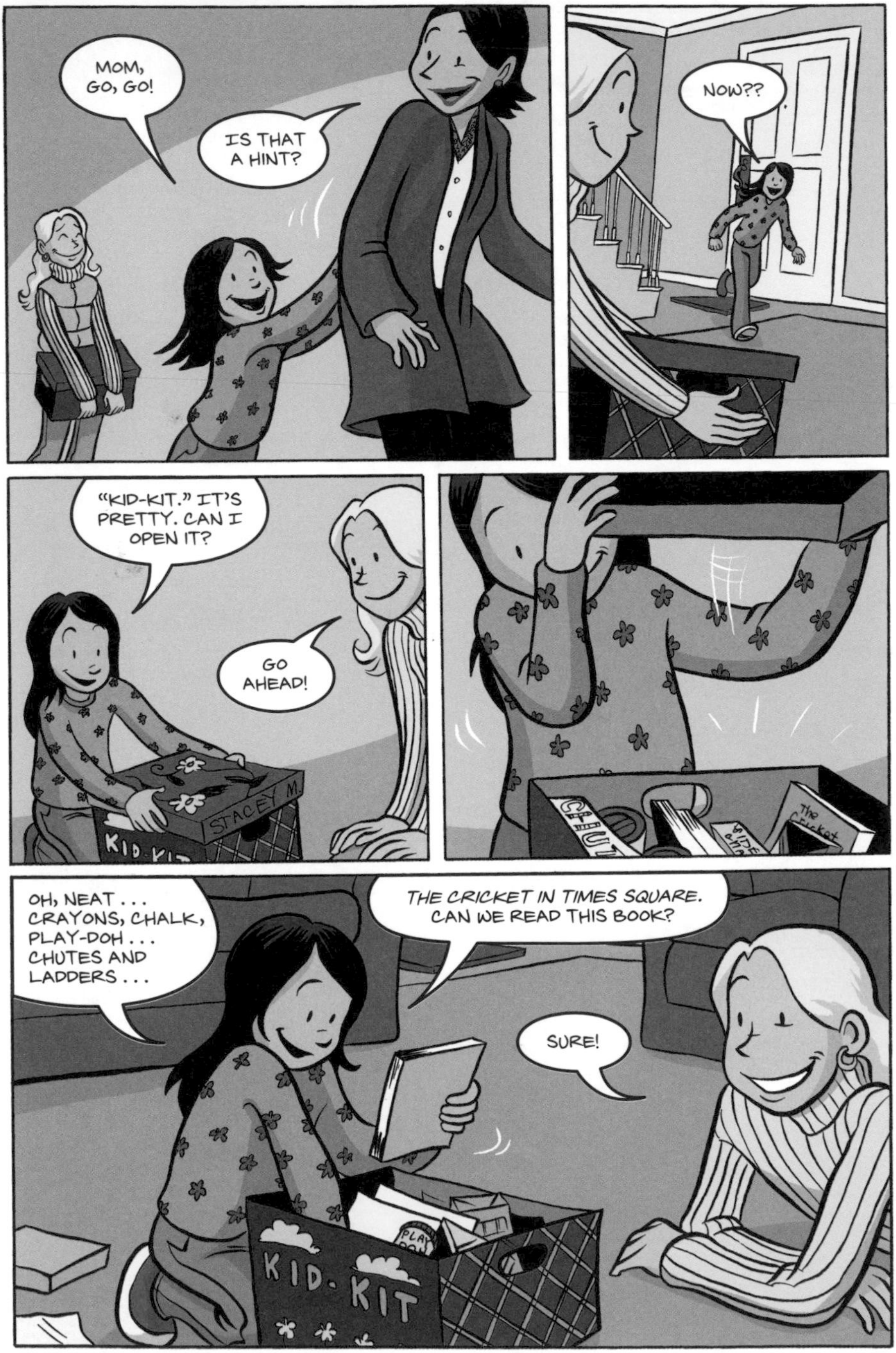
MOM, GO, GO!
IS THAT A HINT?
NOW??
"KID-KIT." IT'S PRETTY. CAN I OPEN IT?
GO AHEAD!
STACEY M.
KID-KIT
OH, NEAT . . . CRAYONS, CHALK, PLAY-DOH . . . CHUTES AND LADDERS . . .
THE CRICKET IN TIMES SQUARE. CAN WE READ THIS BOOK?
SURE!
KID-KIT

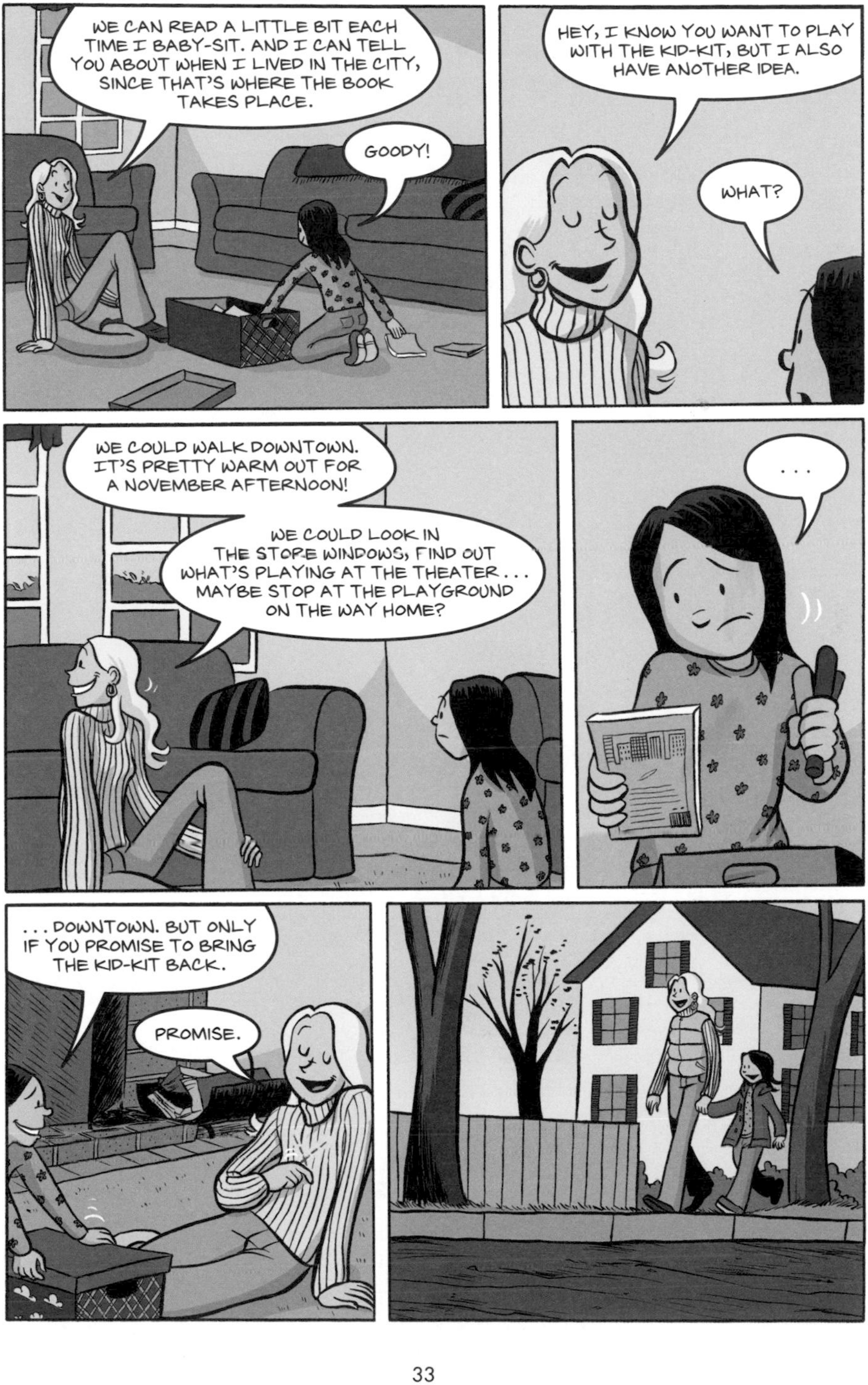
WE CAN READ A LITTLE BIT EACH TIME I BABY-SIT. AND I CAN TELL YOU ABOUT WHEN I LIVED IN THE CITY, SINCE THAT'S WHERE THE BOOK TAKES PLACE.
GOODY!
HEY, I KNOW YOU WANT TO PLAY WITH THE KID-KIT, BUT I ALSO HAVE ANOTHER IDEA.
WHAT?
WE COULD WALK DOWNTOWN. IT'S PRETTY WARM OUT FOR A NOVEMBER AFTERNOON!
WE COULD LOOK IN THE STORE WINDOWS, FIND OUT WHAT'S PLAYING AT THE THEATER . . . MAYBE STOP AT THE PLAYGROUND ON THE WAY HOME?
. . .
. . . DOWNTOWN. BUT ONLY IF YOU PROMISE TO BRING THE KID-KIT BACK.
PROMISE.

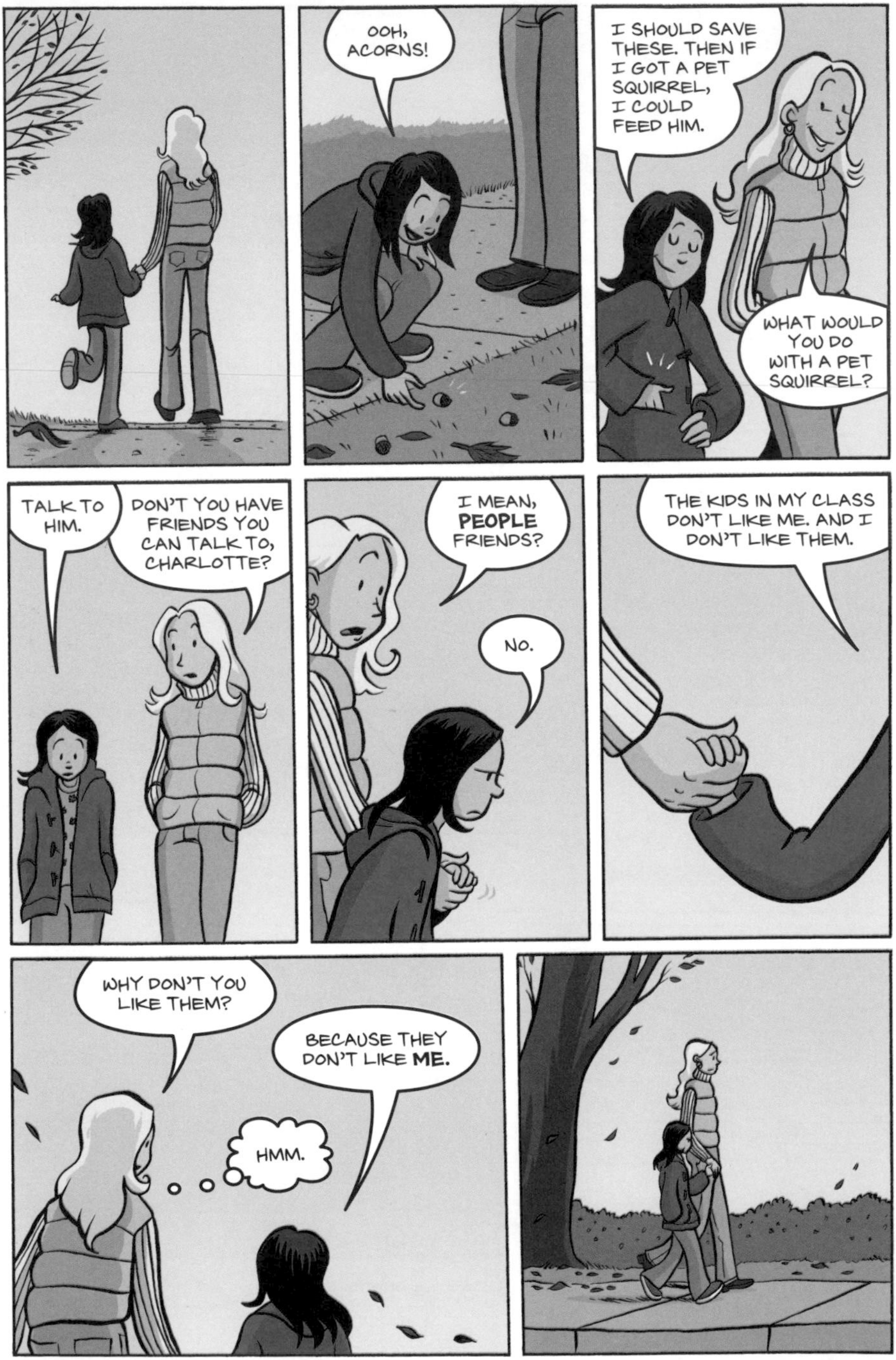
OOH, ACORNS!
I SHOULD SAVE THESE. THEN IF I GOT A PET SQUIRREL, I COULD FEED HIM.
WHAT WOULD YOU DO WITH A PET SQUIRREL?
TALK TO HIM.
DON'T YOU HAVE FRIENDS YOU CAN TALK TO, CHARLOTTE?
I MEAN, **PEOPLE** FRIENDS?
NO.
THE KIDS IN MY CLASS DON'T LIKE ME. AND I DON'T LIKE THEM.
WHY DON'T YOU LIKE THEM?
BECAUSE THEY DON'T LIKE **ME.**
HMM.

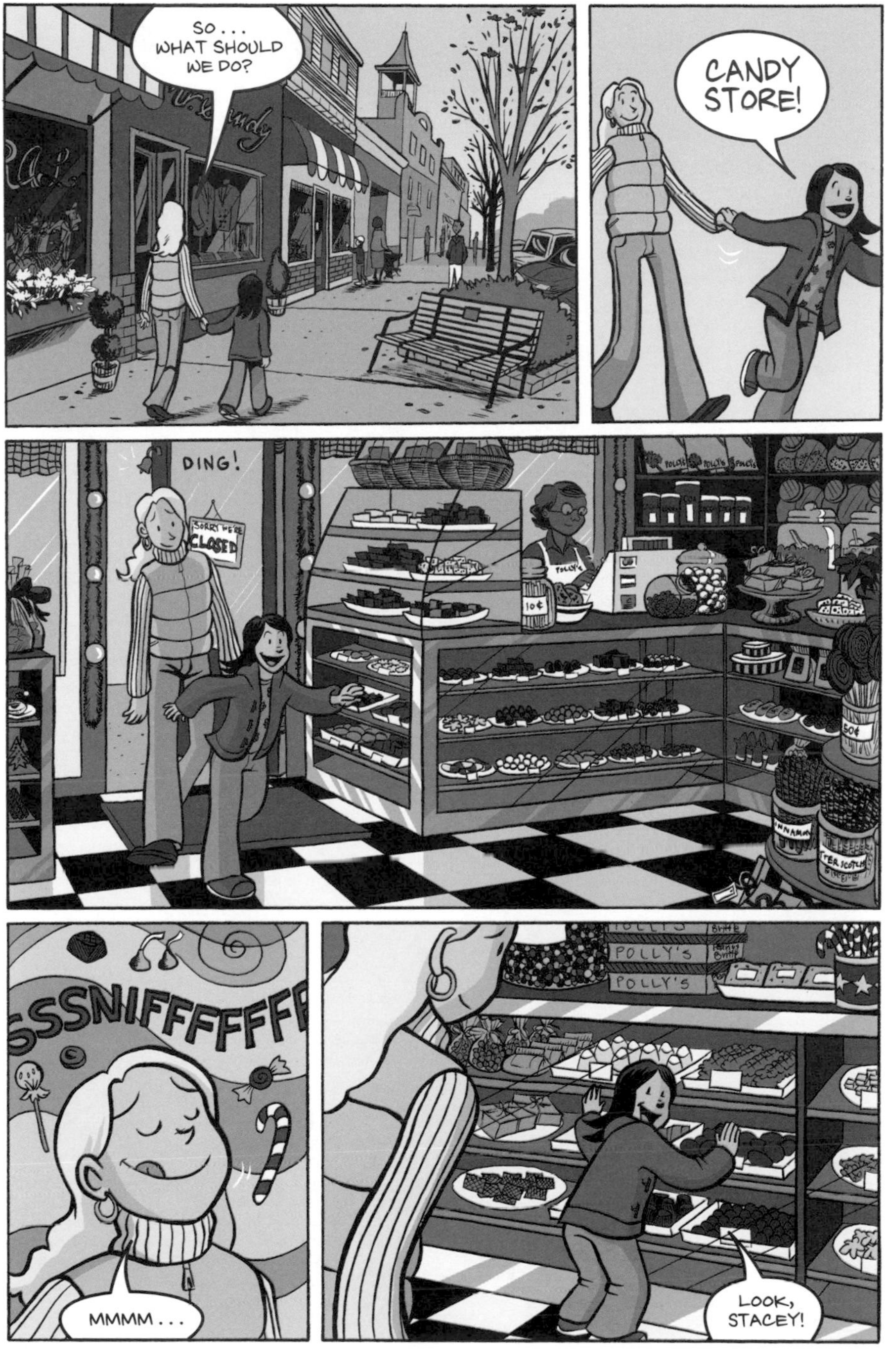
SO . . . WHAT SHOULD WE DO?
CANDY STORE!
DING!
SORRY WE'RE CLOSED
10¢
50¢
SSSNIFFFFFF
MMMM . . .
POLLY'S
POLLY'S
LOOK, STACEY!

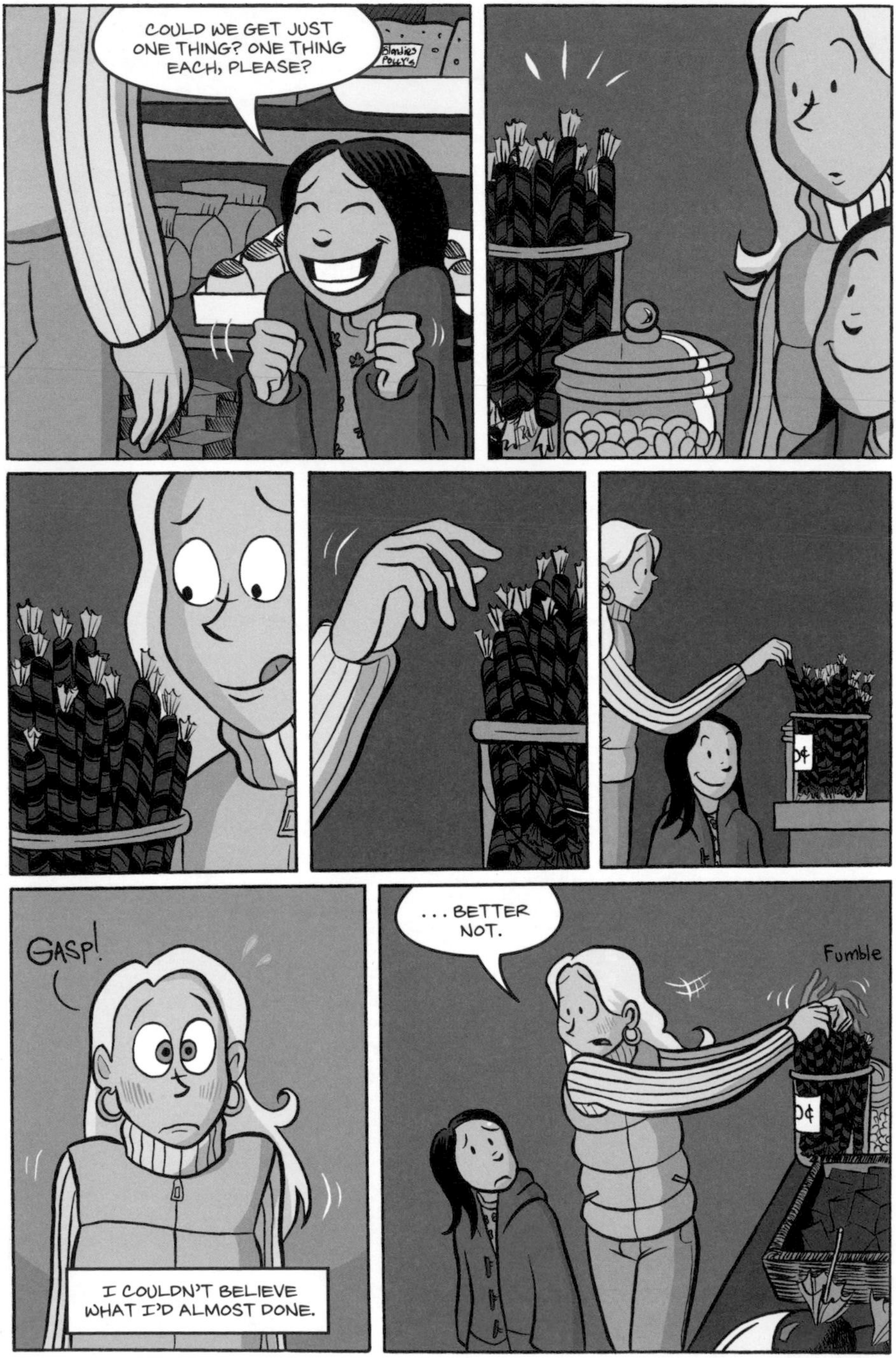
COULD WE GET JUST ONE THING? ONE THING EACH, PLEASE?
GASP!
I COULDN'T BELIEVE WHAT I'D ALMOST DONE.
. . . BETTER NOT.
Fumble

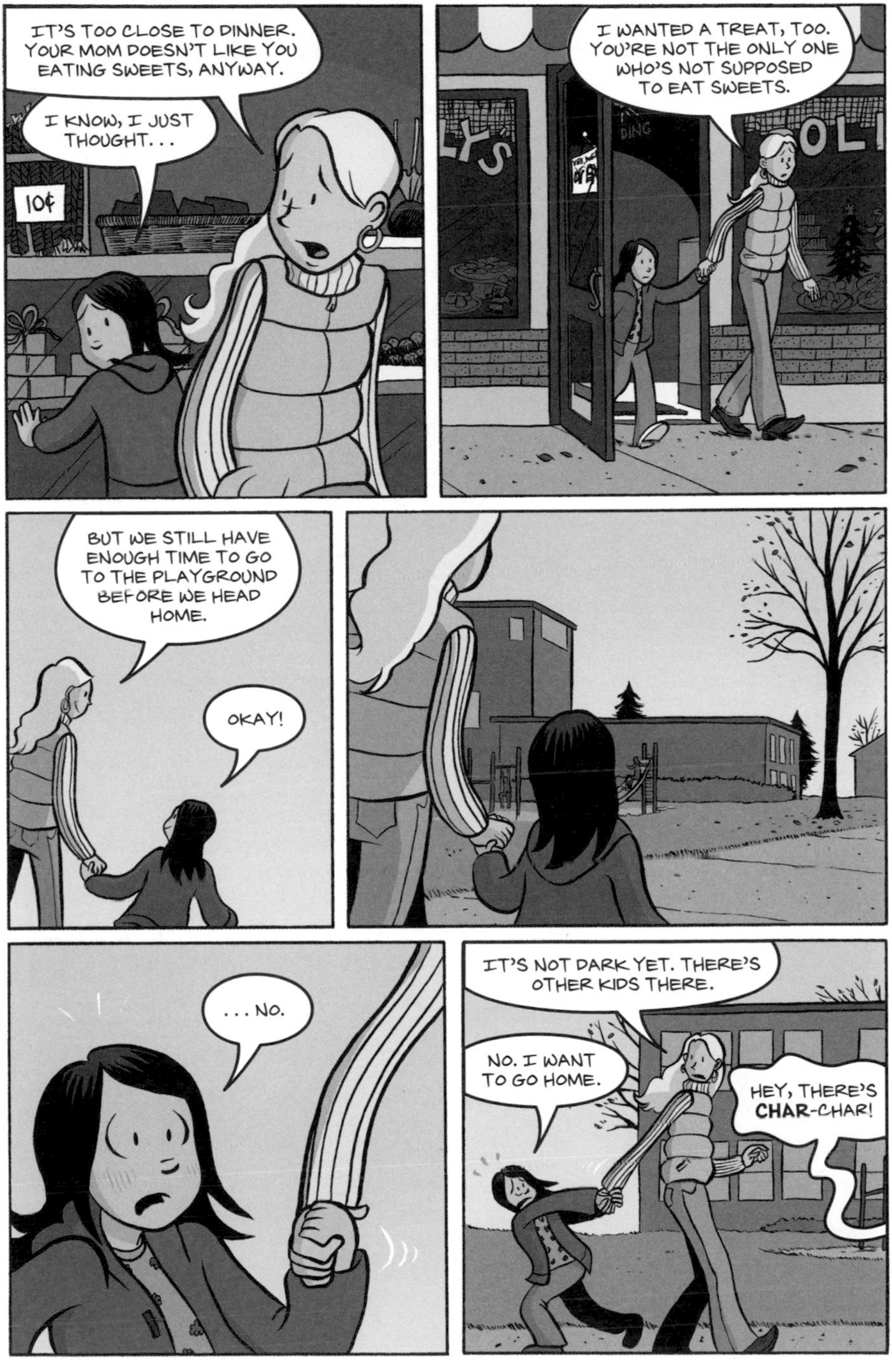
IT'S TOO CLOSE TO DINNER. YOUR MOM DOESN'T LIKE YOU EATING SWEETS, ANYWAY.
I KNOW, I JUST THOUGHT. . .
10¢
I WANTED A TREAT, TOO. YOU'RE NOT THE ONLY ONE WHO'S NOT SUPPOSED TO EAT SWEETS.
DING
BUT WE STILL HAVE ENOUGH TIME TO GO TO THE PLAYGROUND BEFORE WE HEAD HOME.
OKAY!
. . . NO.
IT'S NOT DARK YET. THERE'S OTHER KIDS THERE.
NO. I WANT TO GO HOME.
HEY, THERE'S **CHAR**-CHAR!

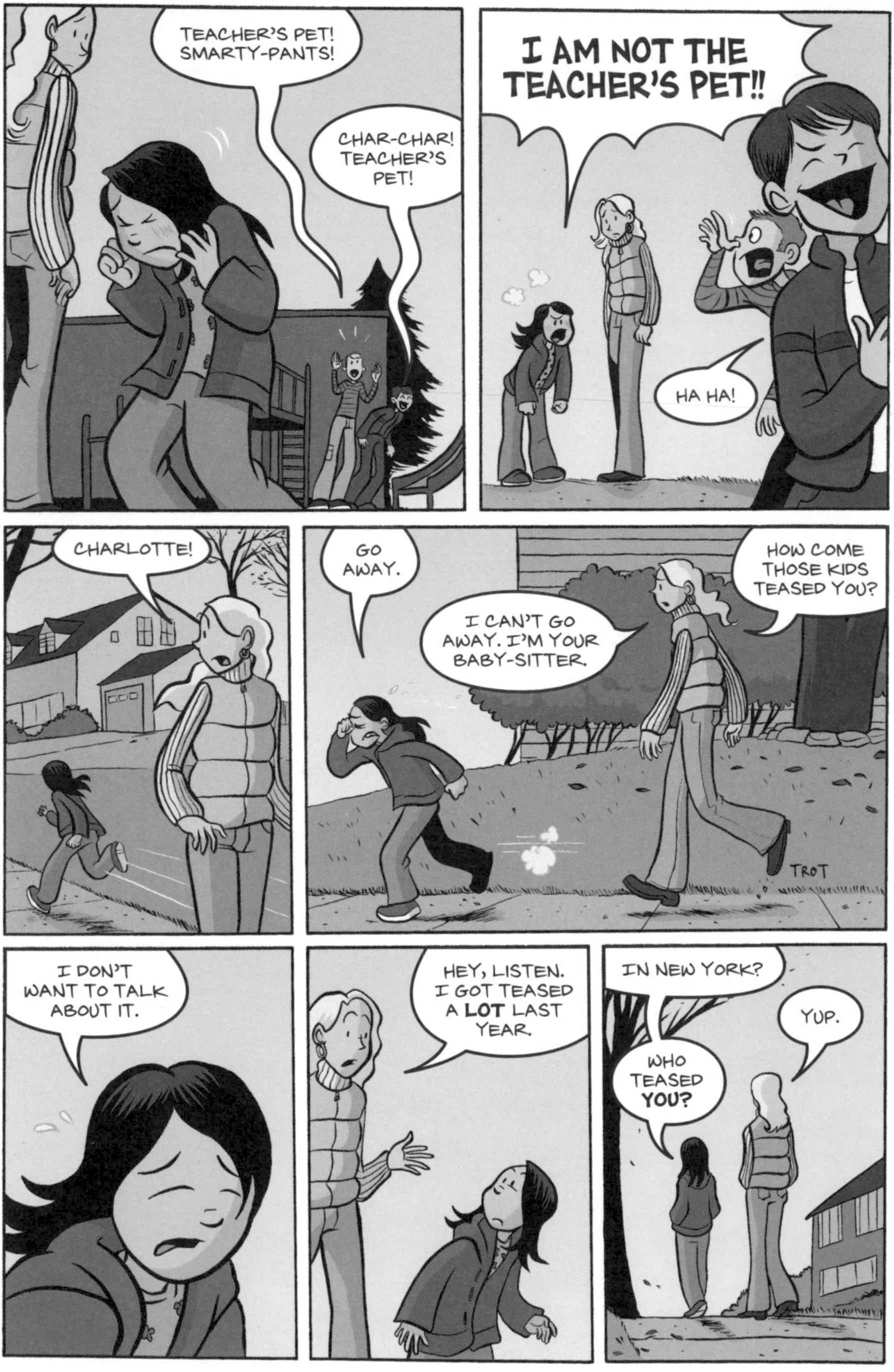
TEACHER'S PET! SMARTY-PANTS!
CHAR-CHAR! TEACHER'S PET!
I AM NOT THE TEACHER'S PET!!
HA HA!
CHARLOTTE!
GO AWAY.
I CAN'T GO AWAY. I'M YOUR BABY-SITTER.
HOW COME THOSE KIDS TEASED YOU?
TROT
I DON'T WANT TO TALK ABOUT IT.
HEY, LISTEN. I GOT TEASED A **LOT** LAST YEAR.
IN NEW YORK?
YUP.
WHO TEASED **YOU?**

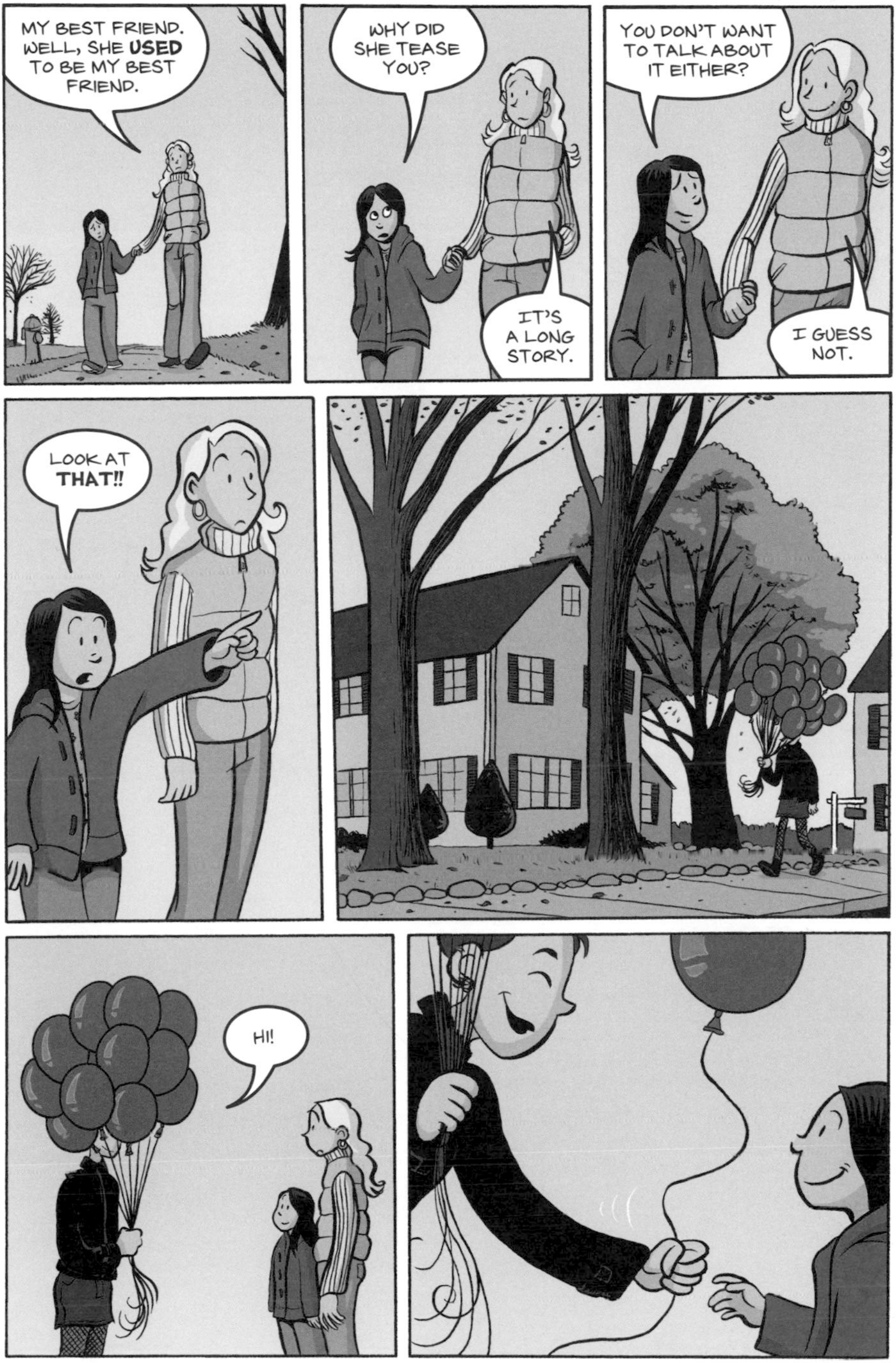
MY BEST FRIEND. WELL, SHE **USED** TO BE MY BEST FRIEND.
WHY DID SHE TEASE YOU?
IT'S A LONG STORY.
YOU DON'T WANT TO TALK ABOUT IT EITHER?
I GUESS NOT.
LOOK AT **THAT!!**
HI!

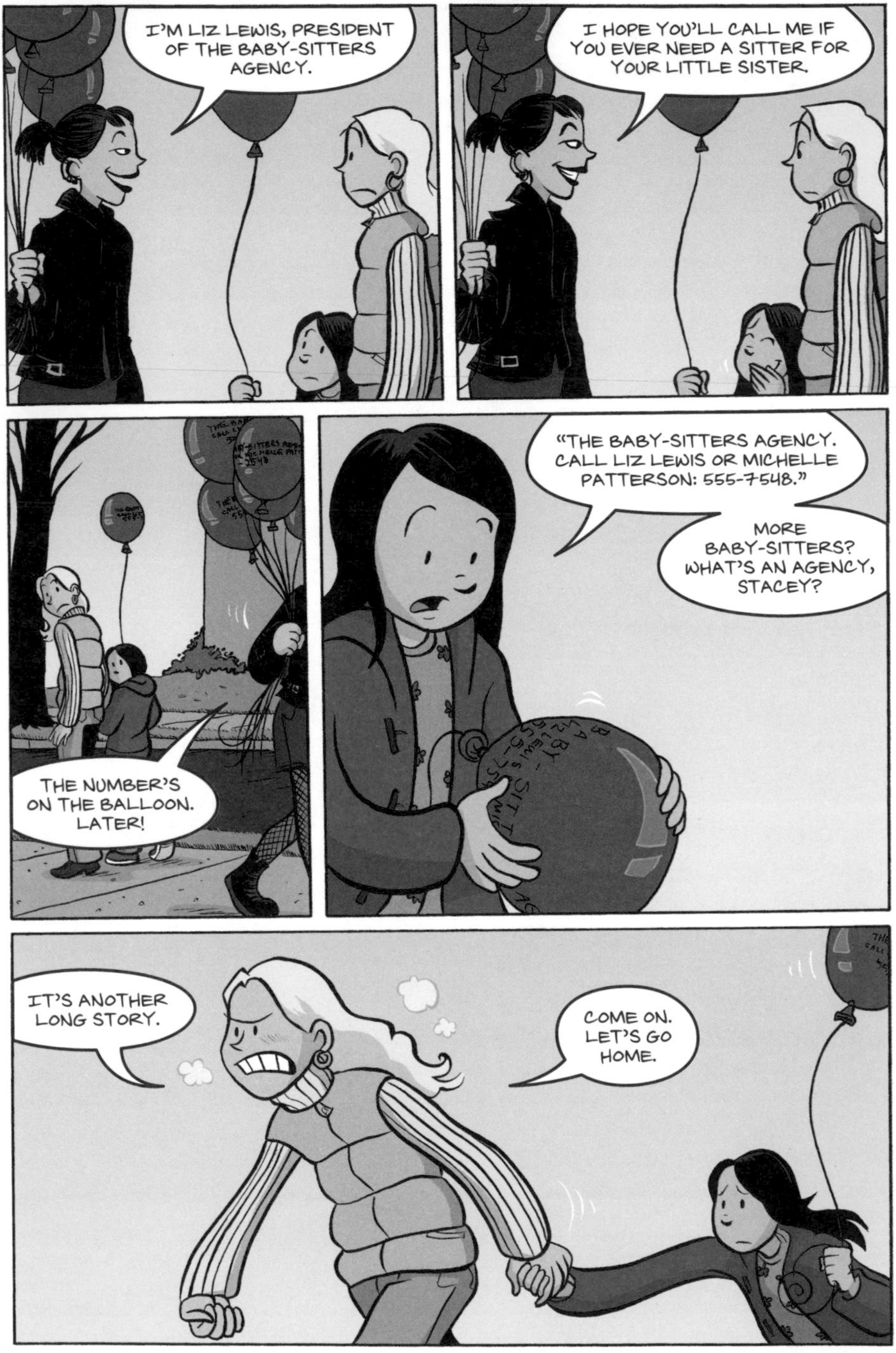
I'M LIZ LEWIS, PRESIDENT OF THE BABY-SITTERS AGENCY.
I HOPE YOU'LL CALL ME IF YOU EVER NEED A SITTER FOR YOUR LITTLE SISTER.
THE NUMBER'S ON THE BALLOON. LATER!
"THE BABY-SITTERS AGENCY. CALL LIZ LEWIS OR MICHELLE PATTERSON: 555-7548."
MORE BABY-SITTERS? WHAT'S AN AGENCY, STACEY?
IT'S ANOTHER LONG STORY.
COME ON. LET'S GO HOME.

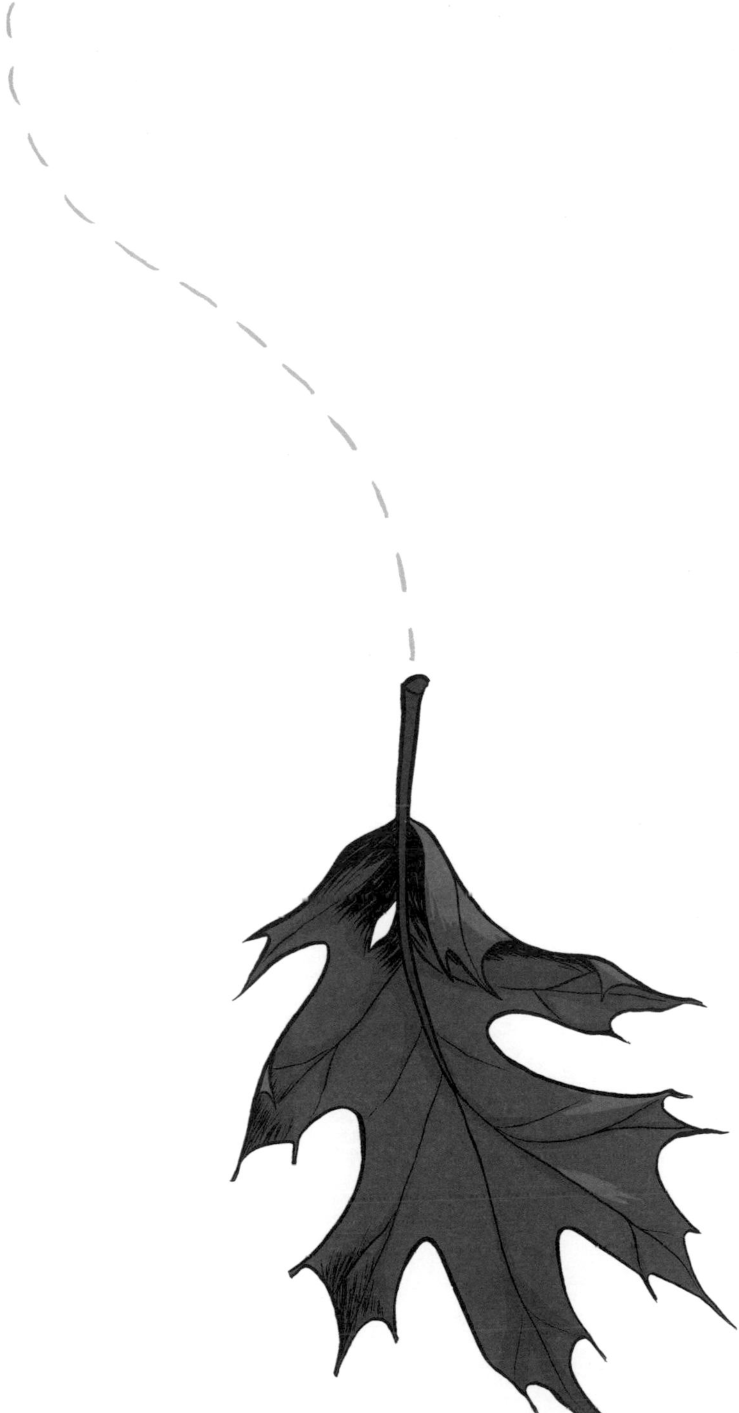

Sunday, November 23

It is just one week since Liz Lewis and Michelle Patterson sent around their fliers. Usually, our club gets about fourteen or fifteen jobs a week. Since last Monday, we've had SEVEN. That's why I'm writing in our notebook. This book is supposed to be a diary of our baby-sitting jobs, so each of us can write up our problems and experiences for the other club members to read. But the Baby-sitters Agency is the biggest problem we've ever had, and I plan to keep track of it in our notebook.

We better do something fast.

— Kristy

CHAPTER 5

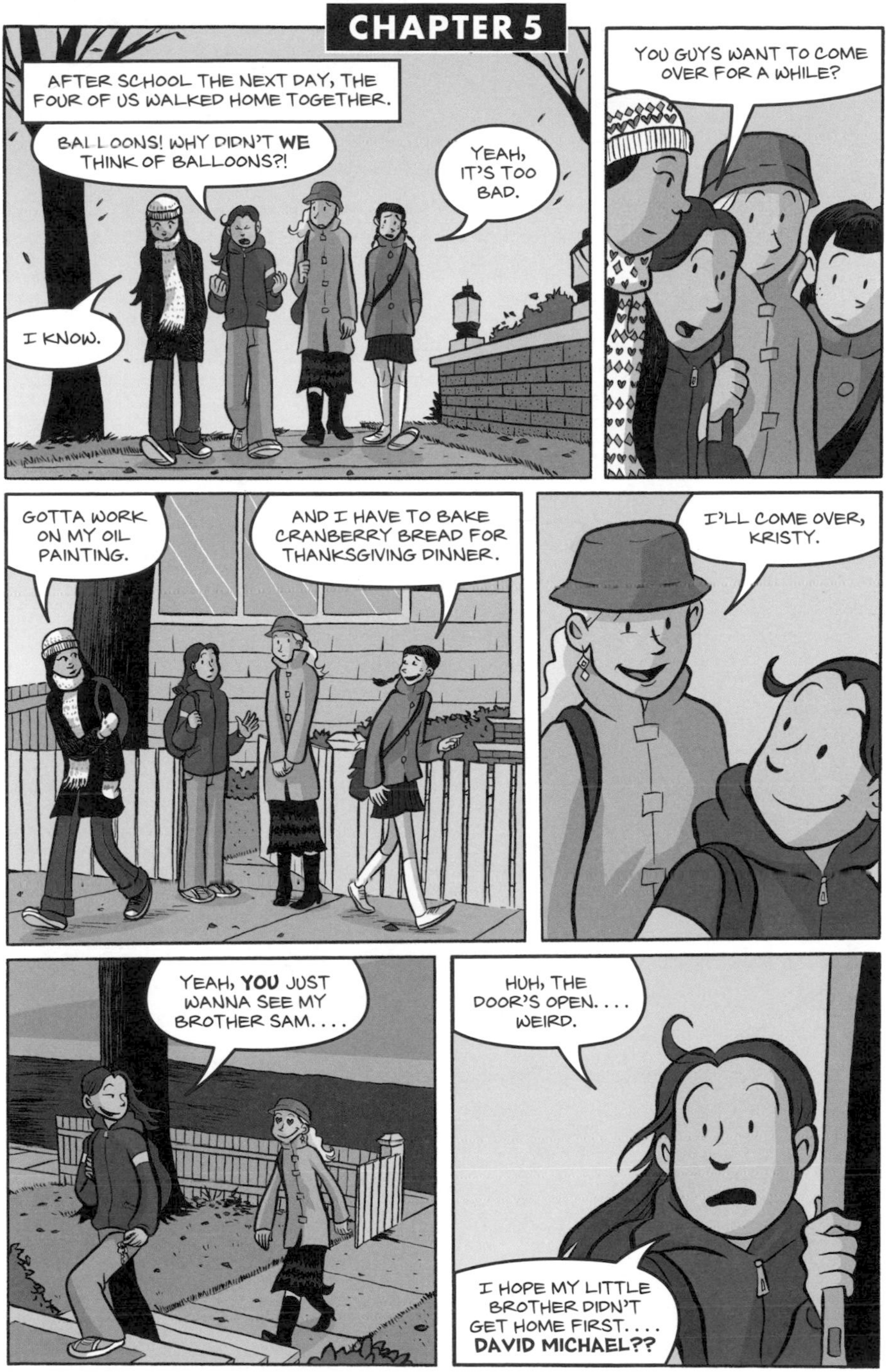
AFTER SCHOOL THE NEXT DAY, THE FOUR OF US WALKED HOME TOGETHER.
BALLOONS! WHY DIDN'T **WE** THINK OF BALLOONS?!
YEAH, IT'S TOO BAD.
I KNOW.
YOU GUYS WANT TO COME OVER FOR A WHILE?
GOTTA WORK ON MY OIL PAINTING.
AND I HAVE TO BAKE CRANBERRY BREAD FOR THANKSGIVING DINNER.
I'LL COME OVER, KRISTY.
YEAH, **YOU** JUST WANNA SEE MY BROTHER SAM....
HUH, THE DOOR'S OPEN.... WEIRD.
I HOPE MY LITTLE BROTHER DIDN'T GET HOME FIRST....
DAVID MICHAEL??

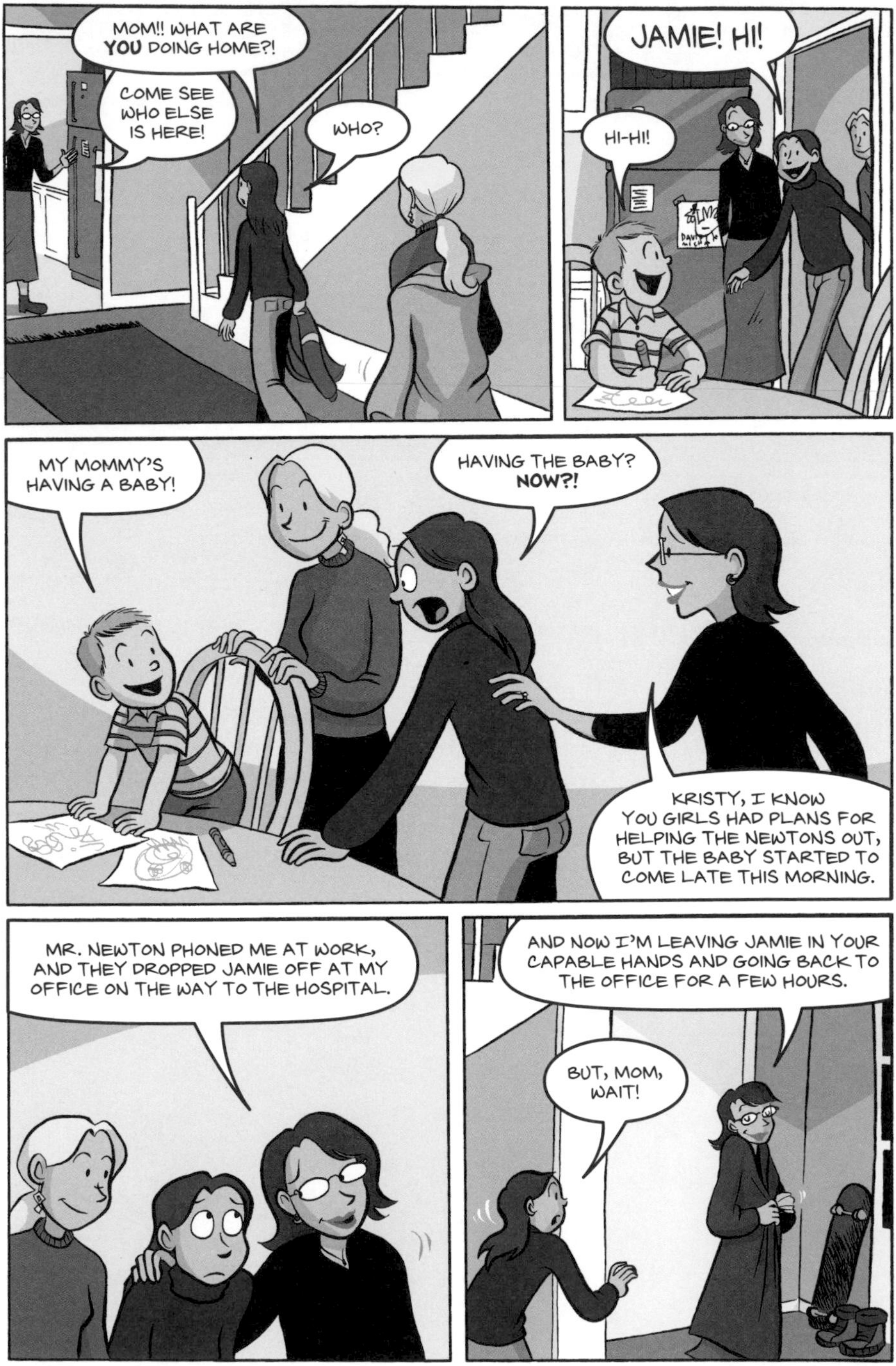
MOM!! WHAT ARE **YOU** DOING HOME?!
COME SEE WHO ELSE IS HERE!
WHO?
JAMIE! HI!
HI-HI!
MY MOMMY'S HAVING A BABY!
HAVING THE BABY? **NOW?!**
KRISTY, I KNOW YOU GIRLS HAD PLANS FOR HELPING THE NEWTONS OUT, BUT THE BABY STARTED TO COME LATE THIS MORNING.
MR. NEWTON PHONED ME AT WORK, AND THEY DROPPED JAMIE OFF AT MY OFFICE ON THE WAY TO THE HOSPITAL.
AND NOW I'M LEAVING JAMIE IN YOUR CAPABLE HANDS AND GOING BACK TO THE OFFICE FOR A FEW HOURS.
BUT, MOM, WAIT!

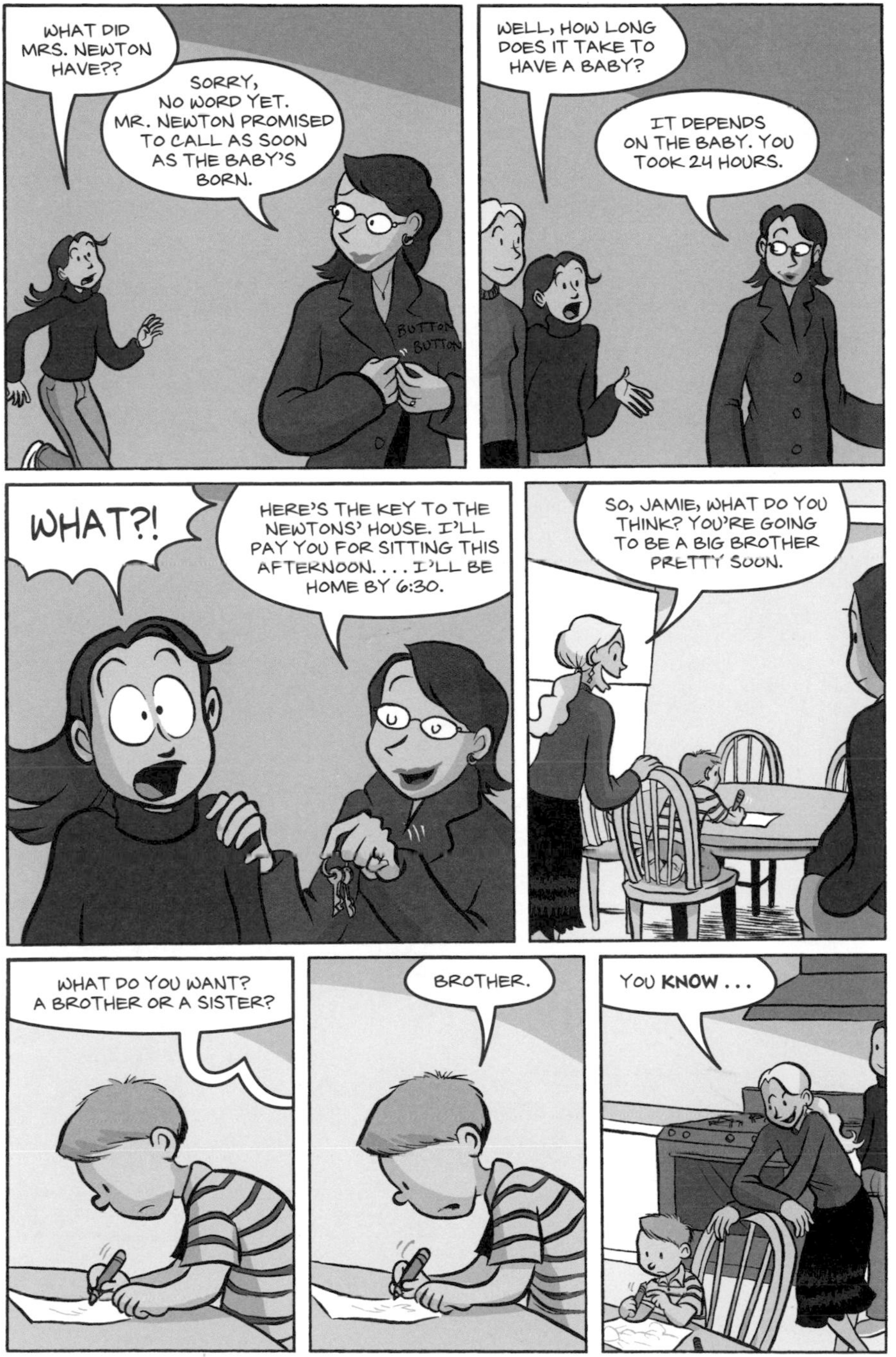
WHAT DID MRS. NEWTON HAVE??
SORRY, NO WORD YET. MR. NEWTON PROMISED TO CALL AS SOON AS THE BABY'S BORN.
BUTTON BUTTON
WELL, HOW LONG DOES IT TAKE TO HAVE A BABY?
IT DEPENDS ON THE BABY. YOU TOOK 24 HOURS.
WHAT?!
HERE'S THE KEY TO THE NEWTONS' HOUSE. I'LL PAY YOU FOR SITTING THIS AFTERNOON. . . . I'LL BE HOME BY 6:30.
SO, JAMIE, WHAT DO YOU THINK? YOU'RE GOING TO BE A BIG BROTHER PRETTY SOON.
WHAT DO YOU WANT? A BROTHER OR A SISTER?
BROTHER.
YOU **KNOW** . . .

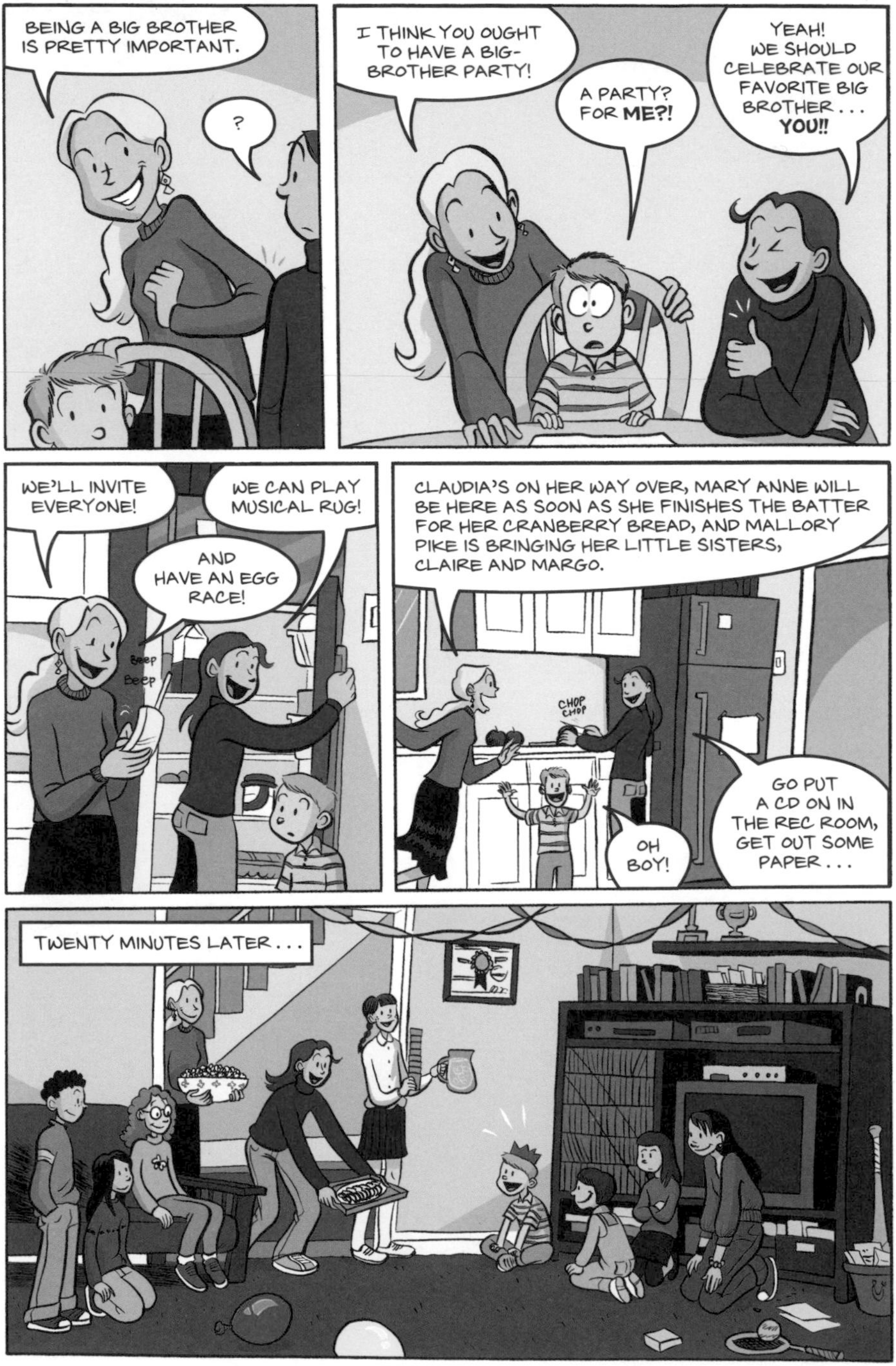
BEING A BIG BROTHER IS PRETTY IMPORTANT.
?
I THINK YOU OUGHT TO HAVE A BIG-BROTHER PARTY!
A PARTY? FOR **ME?!**
YEAH! WE SHOULD CELEBRATE OUR FAVORITE BIG BROTHER . . . **YOU!!**
WE'LL INVITE EVERYONE!
WE CAN PLAY MUSICAL RUG!
AND HAVE AN EGG RACE!
BEEP BEEP
CLAUDIA'S ON HER WAY OVER, MARY ANNE WILL BE HERE AS SOON AS SHE FINISHES THE BATTER FOR HER CRANBERRY BREAD, AND MALLORY PIKE IS BRINGING HER LITTLE SISTERS, CLAIRE AND MARGO.
CHOP CHOP
OH BOY!
GO PUT A CD ON IN THE REC ROOM, GET OUT SOME PAPER . . .
TWENTY MINUTES LATER . . .

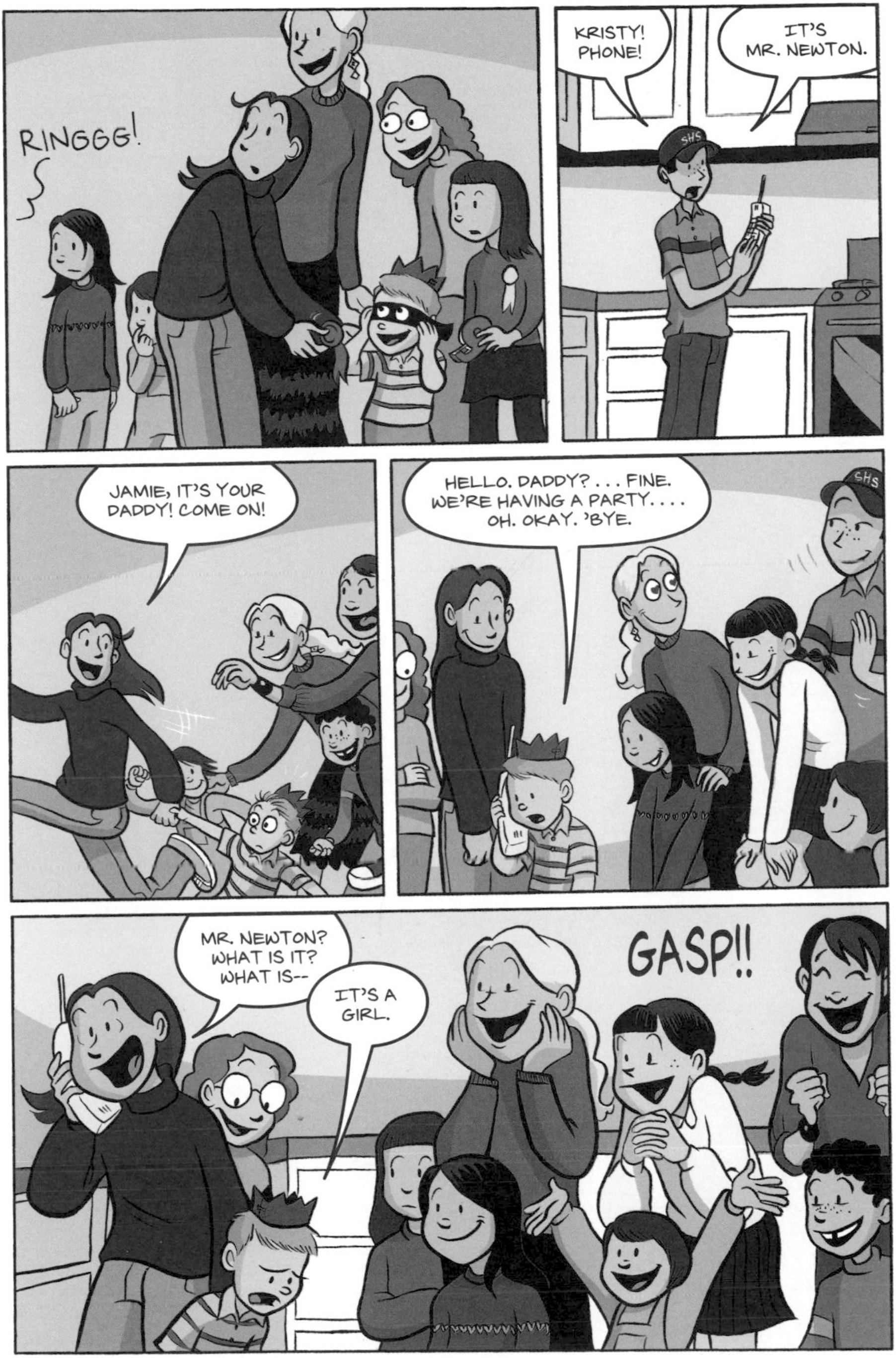

RINGGG!
KRISTY! PHONE!
IT'S MR. NEWTON.
JAMIE, IT'S YOUR DADDY! COME ON!
HELLO. DADDY? . . . FINE. WE'RE HAVING A PARTY. . . . OH. OKAY. 'BYE.
MR. NEWTON? WHAT IS IT? WHAT IS--
IT'S A GIRL.
GASP!!

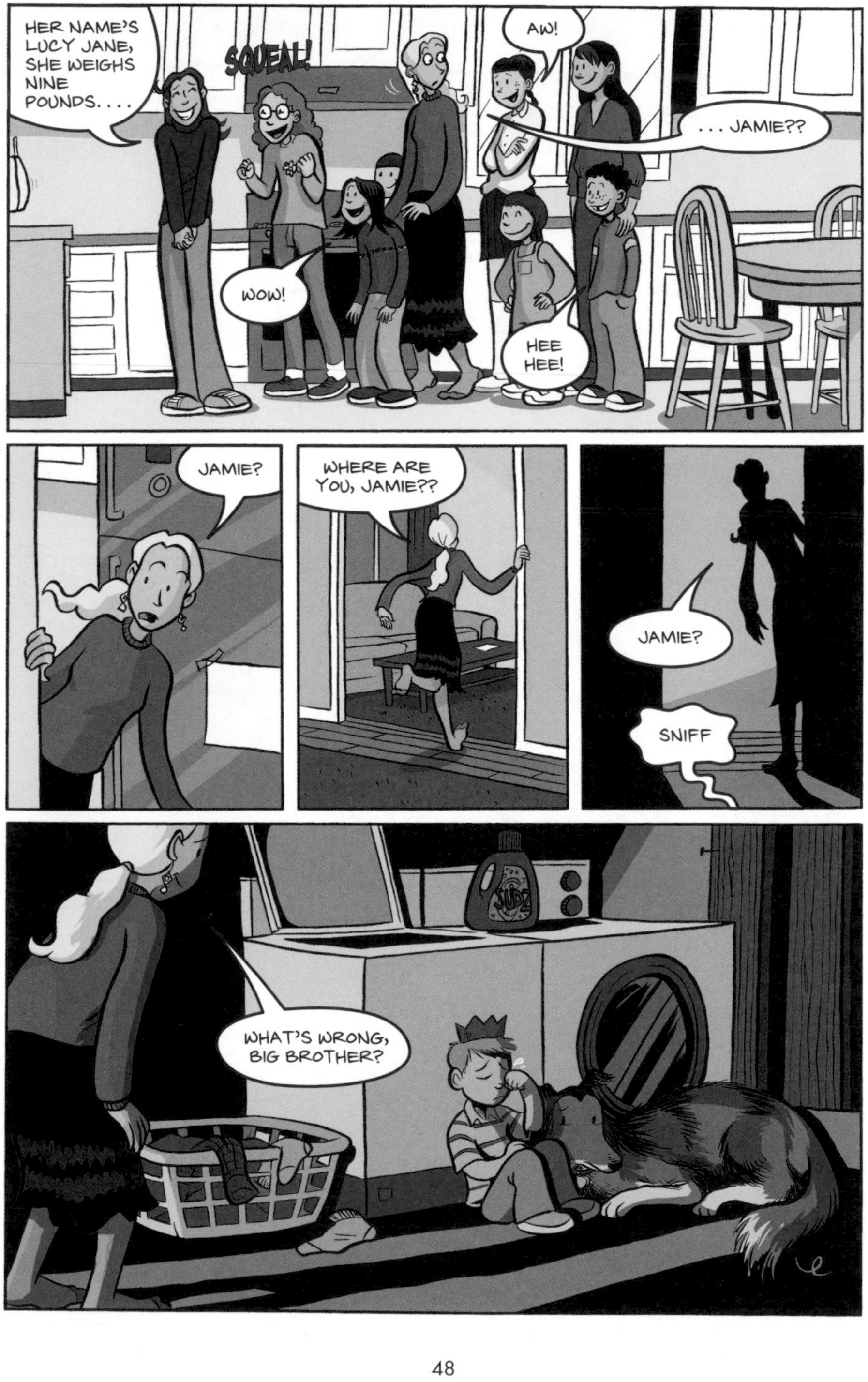
HER NAME'S LUCY JANE, SHE WEIGHS NINE POUNDS. . . .
SQUEAL!
AW!
. . . JAMIE??
WOW!
HEE HEE!
JAMIE?
WHERE ARE YOU, JAMIE??
JAMIE?
SNIFF
SUDZ
WHAT'S WRONG, BIG BROTHER?

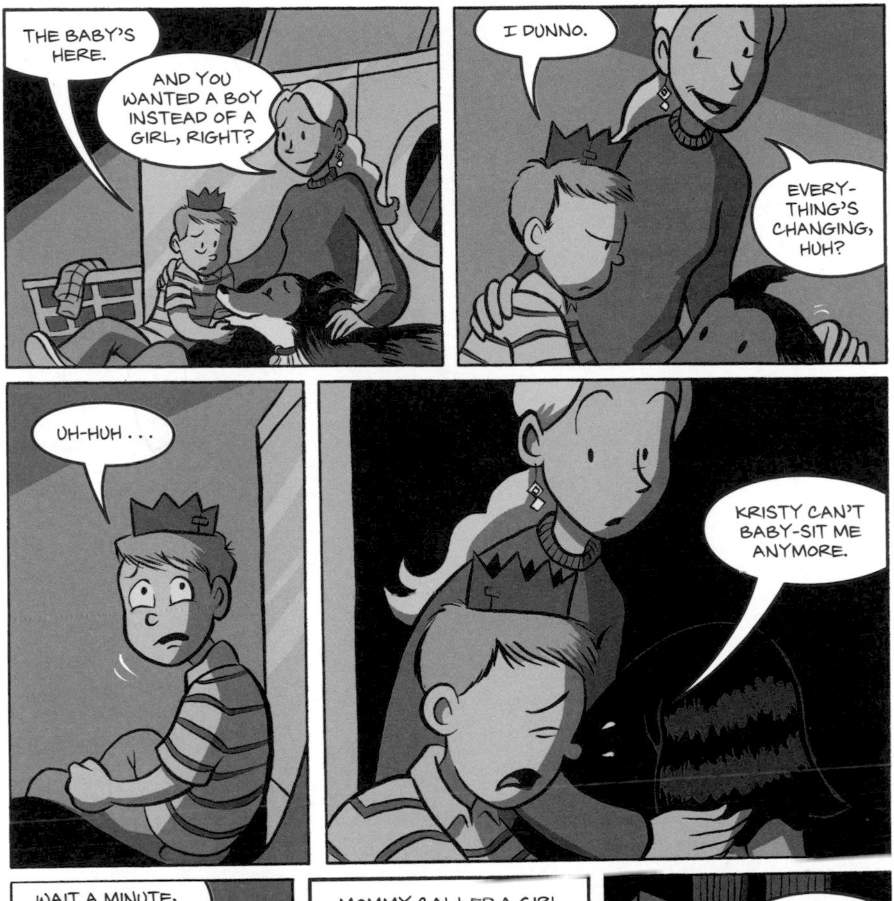
THE BABY'S HERE.
AND YOU WANTED A BOY INSTEAD OF A GIRL, RIGHT?
I DUNNO.
EVERY-THING'S CHANGING, HUH?
UH-HUH . . .
KRISTY CAN'T BABY-SIT ME ANYMORE.
WAIT A MINUTE, JAMIE . . . WHAT DO YOU MEAN??
MOMMY CALLED A GIRL AND SAID, "WE NEED AN OLDER SITTER FOR THE NEW BABY."
WAS THE GIRL NAMED LIZ LEWIS?

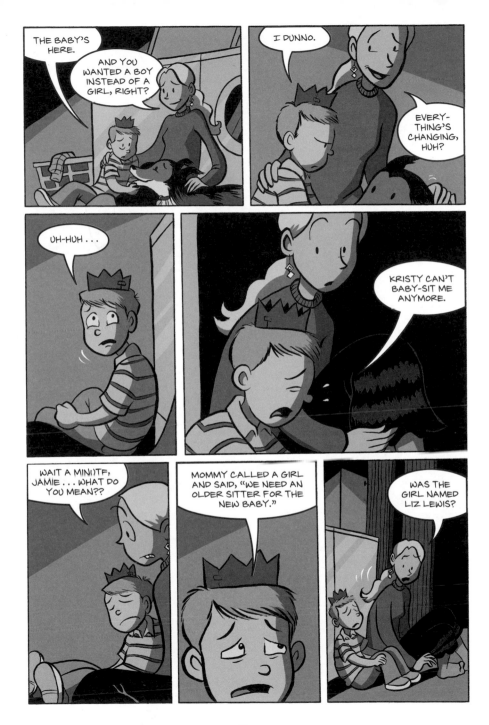

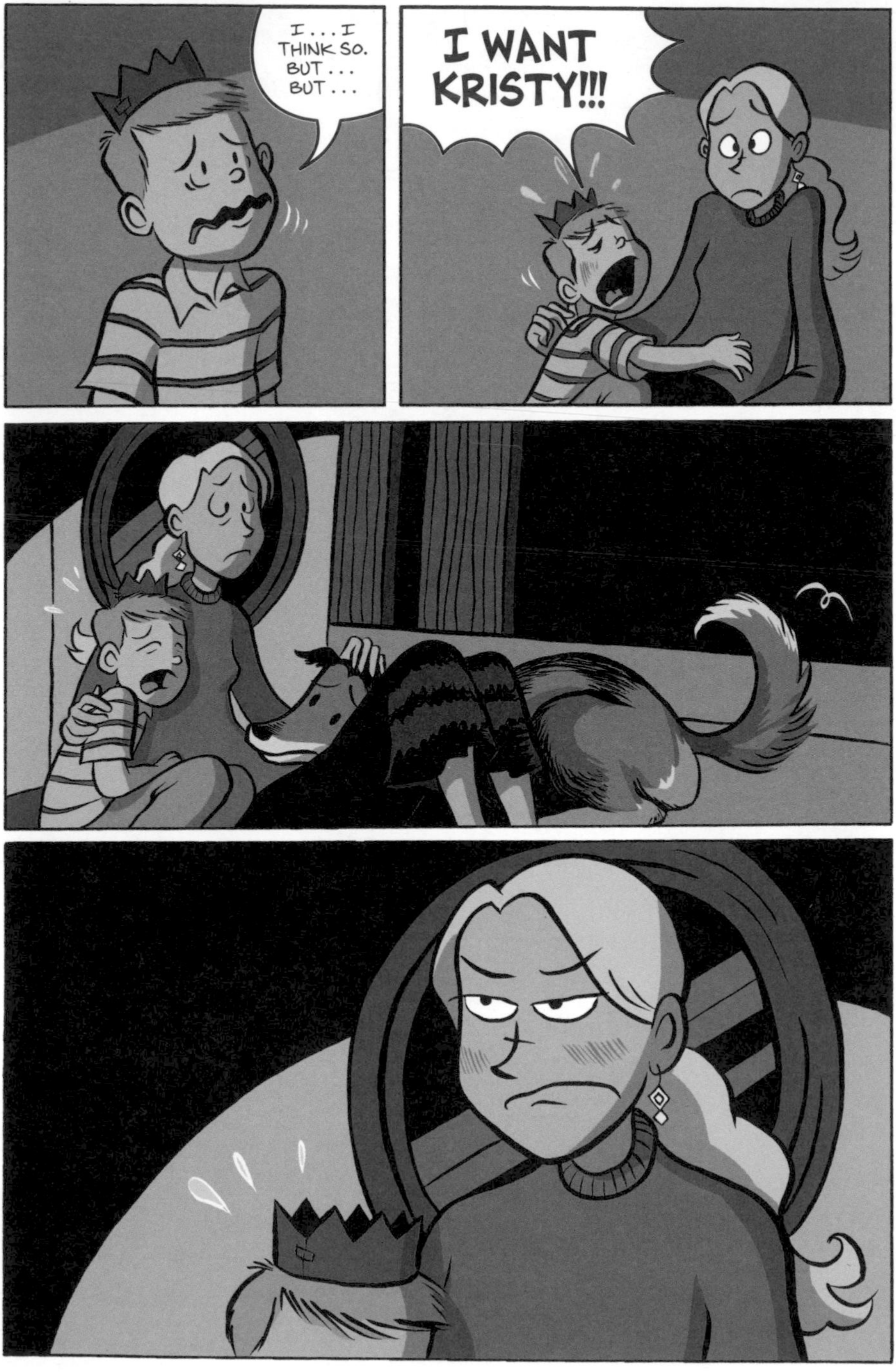
I . . . I THINK SO. BUT . . . BUT . . .
I WANT KRISTY!!!

CHAPTER 6

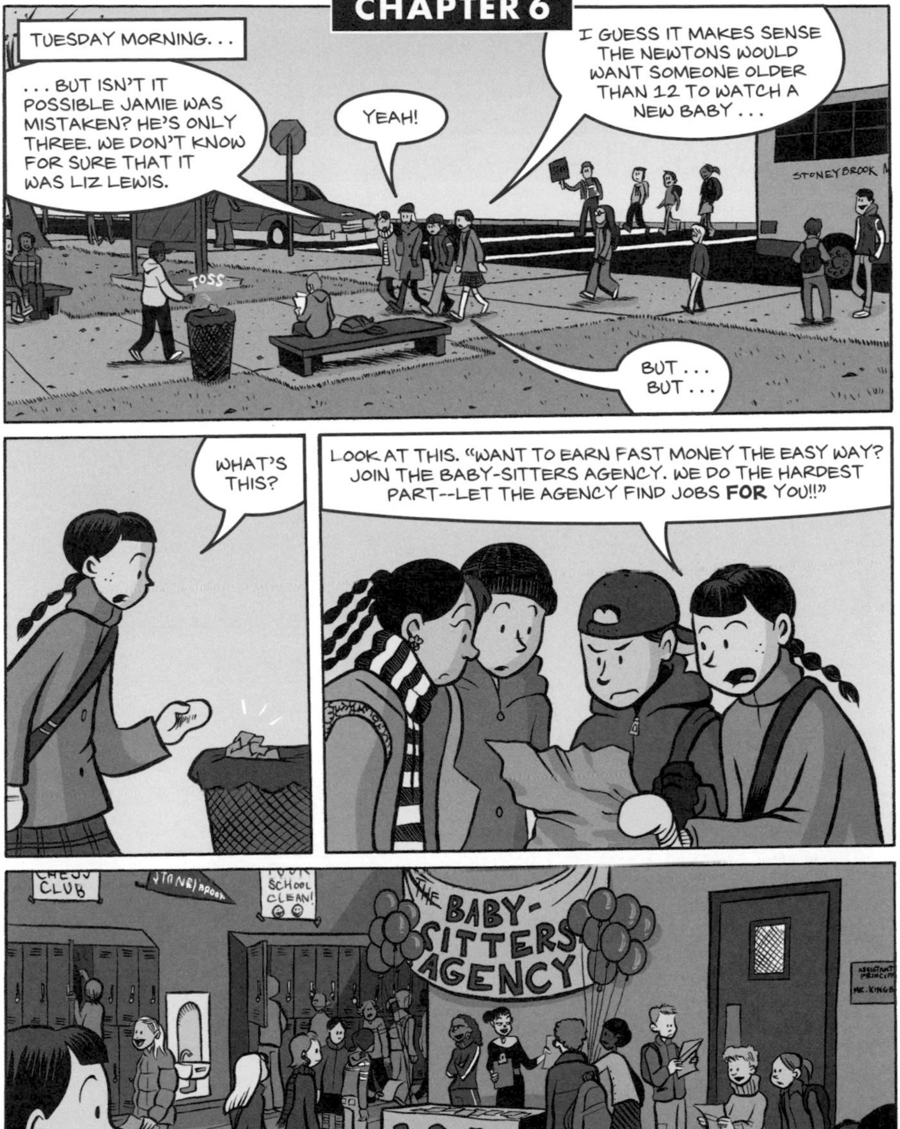

TUESDAY MORNING. . .
. . . BUT ISN'T IT POSSIBLE JAMIE WAS MISTAKEN? HE'S ONLY THREE. WE DON'T KNOW FOR SURE THAT IT WAS LIZ LEWIS.
YEAH!
I GUESS IT MAKES SENSE THE NEWTONS WOULD WANT SOMEONE OLDER THAN 12 TO WATCH A NEW BABY . . .
BUT . . . BUT . . .
STONEYBROOK
TOSS
WHAT'S THIS?
LOOK AT THIS. "WANT TO EARN FAST MONEY THE EASY WAY? JOIN THE BABY-SITTERS AGENCY. WE DO THE HARDEST PART--LET THE AGENCY FIND JOBS **FOR** YOU!!"
CLUB
SCHOOL CLEAN!
THE BABY-SITTERS AGENCY
BSA
STONEY BROOK

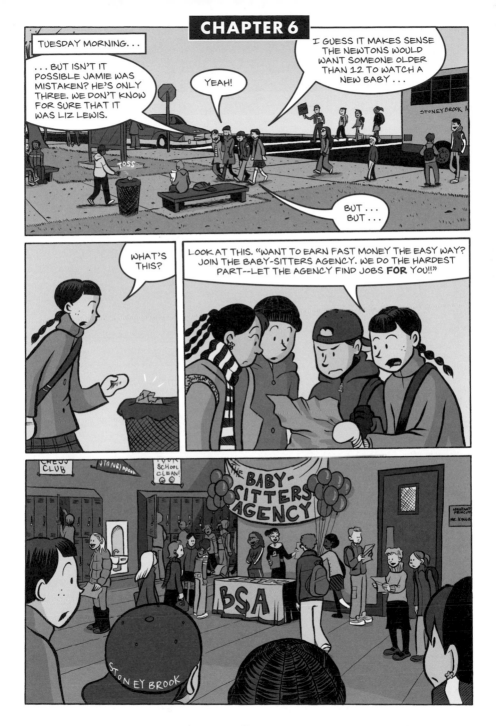

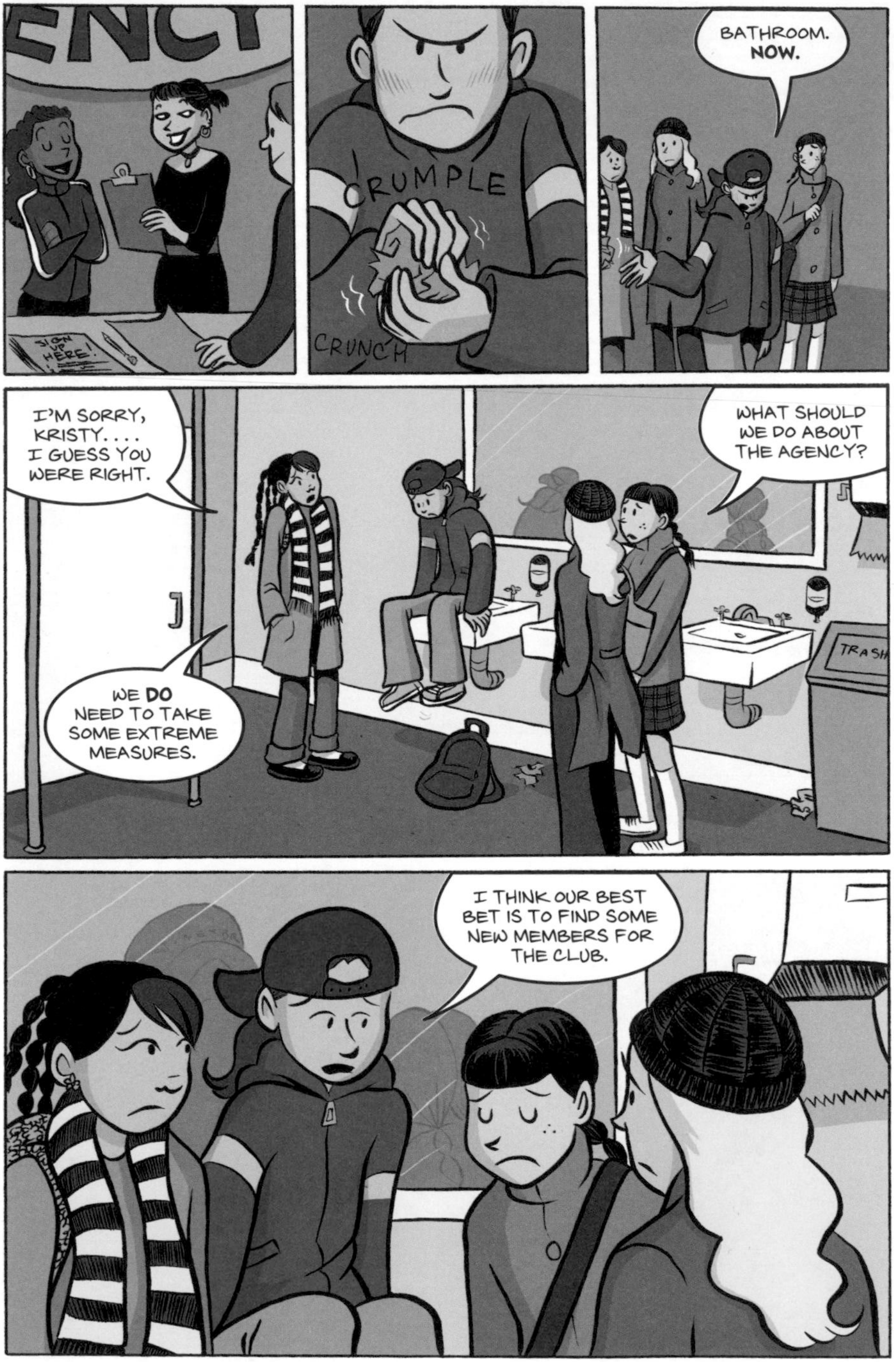
ENCY
SIGN UP HERE!
CRUMPLE
CRUNCH
BATHROOM. **NOW.**
I'M SORRY, KRISTY. . . . I GUESS YOU WERE RIGHT.
WHAT SHOULD WE DO ABOUT THE AGENCY?
WE **DO** NEED TO TAKE SOME EXTREME MEASURES.
TRASH
I THINK OUR BEST BET IS TO FIND SOME NEW MEMBERS FOR THE CLUB.

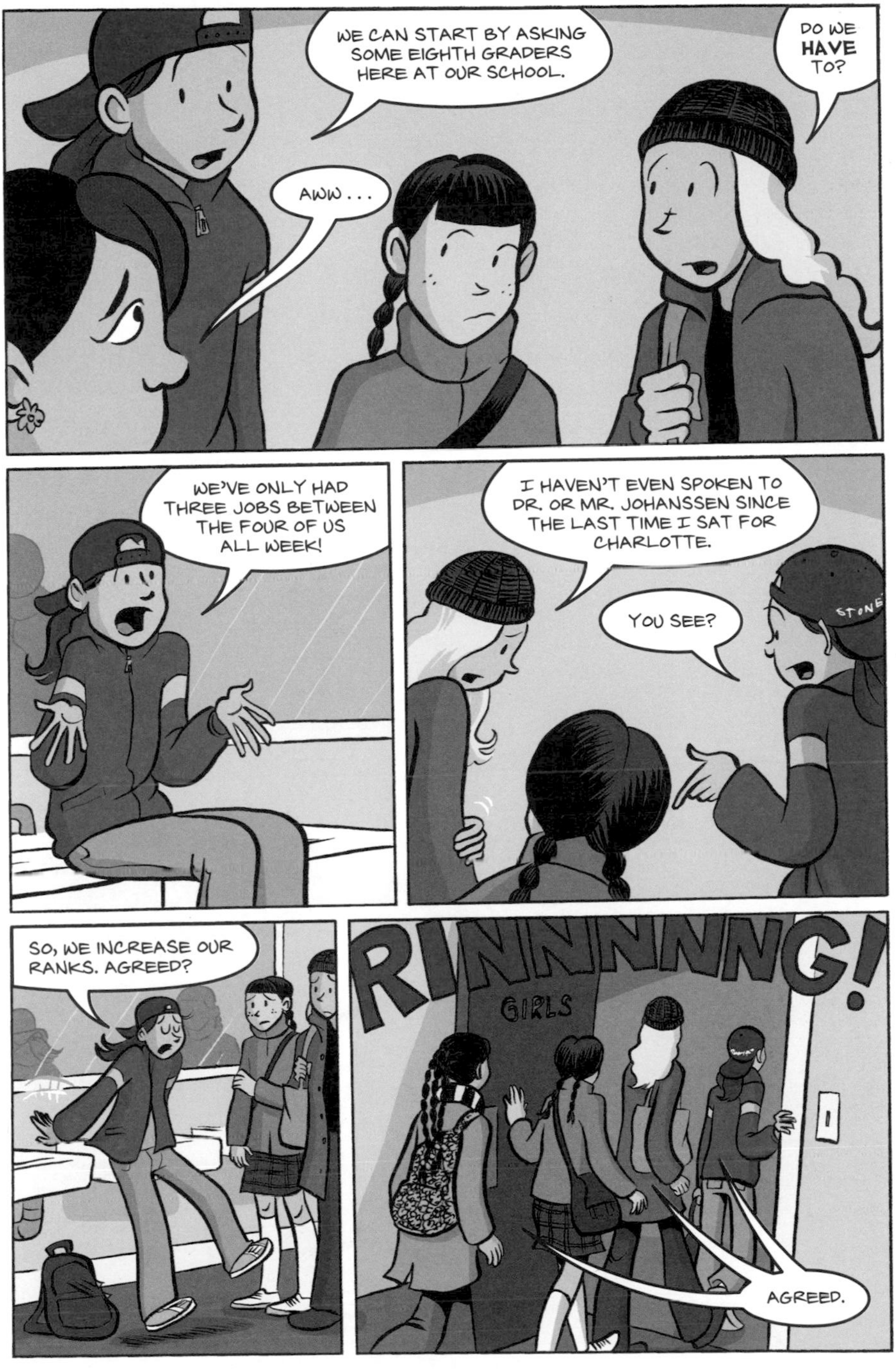
WE CAN START BY ASKING SOME EIGHTH GRADERS HERE AT OUR SCHOOL.
DO WE HAVE TO?
AWW . . .
WE'VE ONLY HAD THREE JOBS BETWEEN THE FOUR OF US ALL WEEK!
I HAVEN'T EVEN SPOKEN TO DR. OR MR. JOHANSSEN SINCE THE LAST TIME I SAT FOR CHARLOTTE.
YOU SEE?
STONE
SO, WE INCREASE OUR RANKS. AGREED?
RINNNNNG!
GIRLS
AGREED.

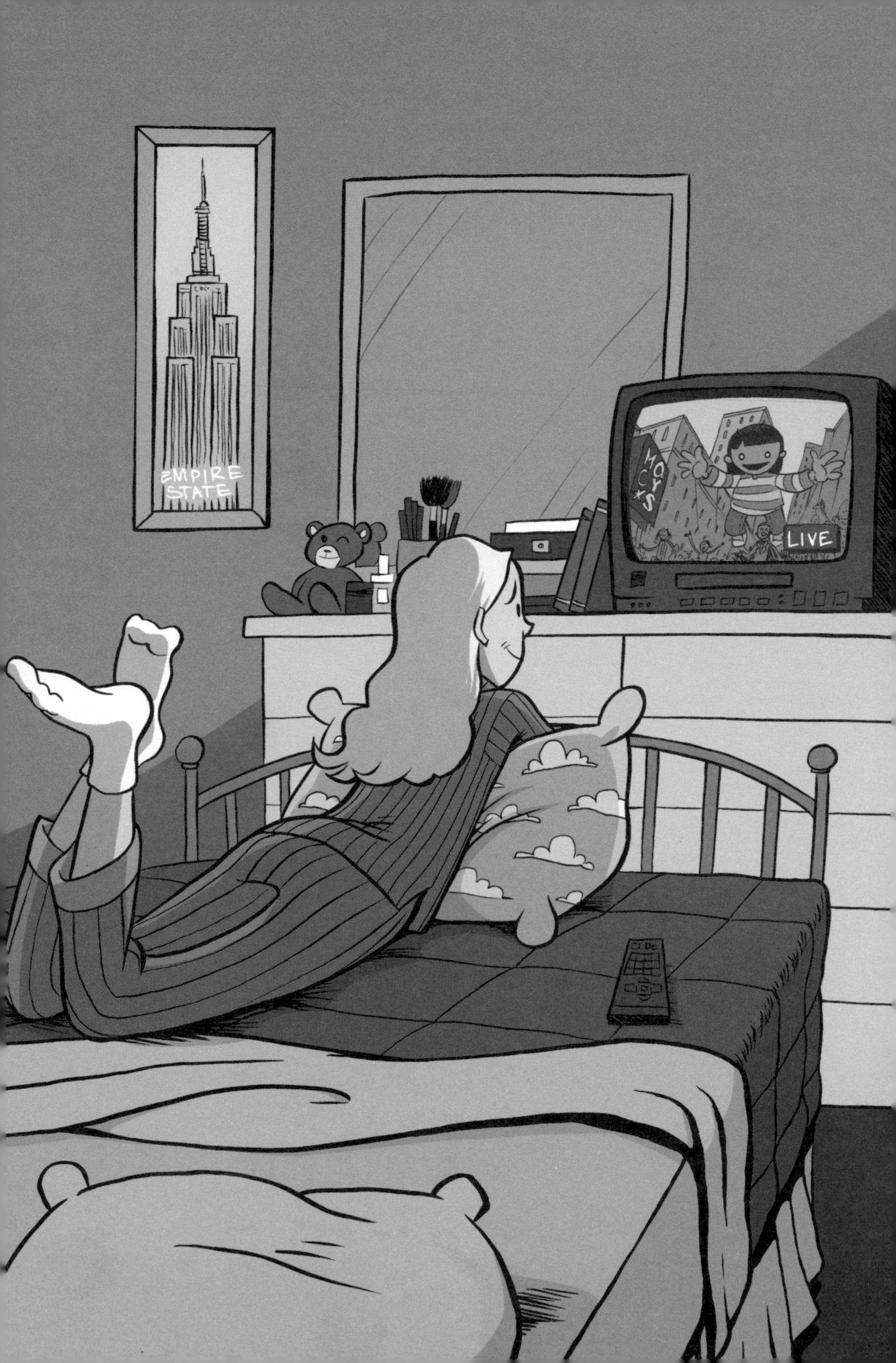
EMPIRE
STATE
LIVE

CHAPTER 7

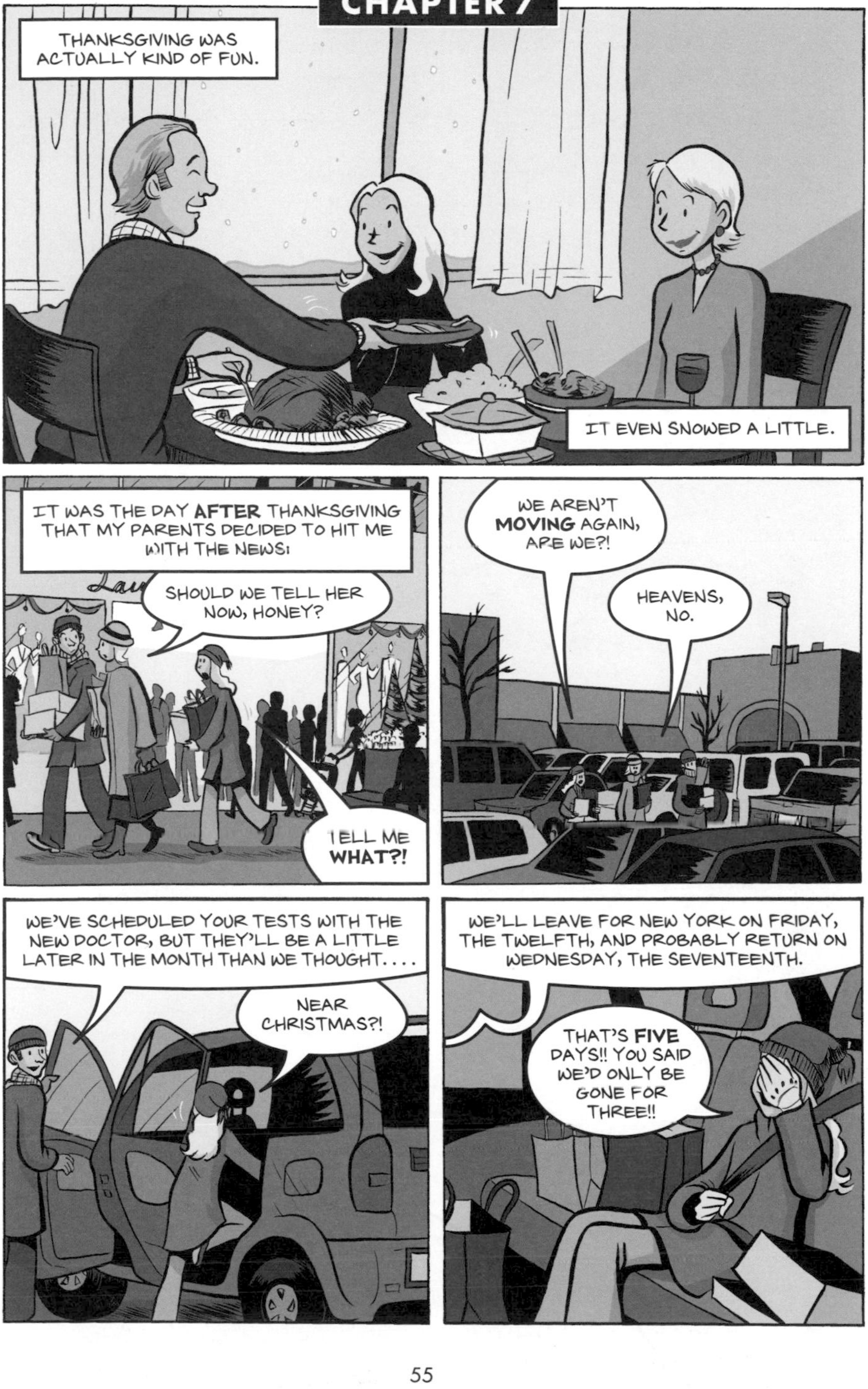
THANKSGIVING WAS ACTUALLY KIND OF FUN.
IT EVEN SNOWED A LITTLE.
IT WAS THE DAY **AFTER** THANKSGIVING THAT MY PARENTS DECIDED TO HIT ME WITH THE NEWS:
SHOULD WE TELL HER NOW, HONEY?
TELL ME **WHAT?!**
WE AREN'T **MOVING** AGAIN, ARE WE?!
HEAVENS, NO.
WE'VE SCHEDULED YOUR TESTS WITH THE NEW DOCTOR, BUT THEY'LL BE A LITTLE LATER IN THE MONTH THAN WE THOUGHT. . . .
NEAR CHRISTMAS?!
WE'LL LEAVE FOR NEW YORK ON FRIDAY, THE TWELFTH, AND PROBABLY RETURN ON WEDNESDAY, THE SEVENTEENTH.
THAT'S **FIVE** DAYS!! YOU SAID WE'D ONLY BE GONE FOR THREE!!

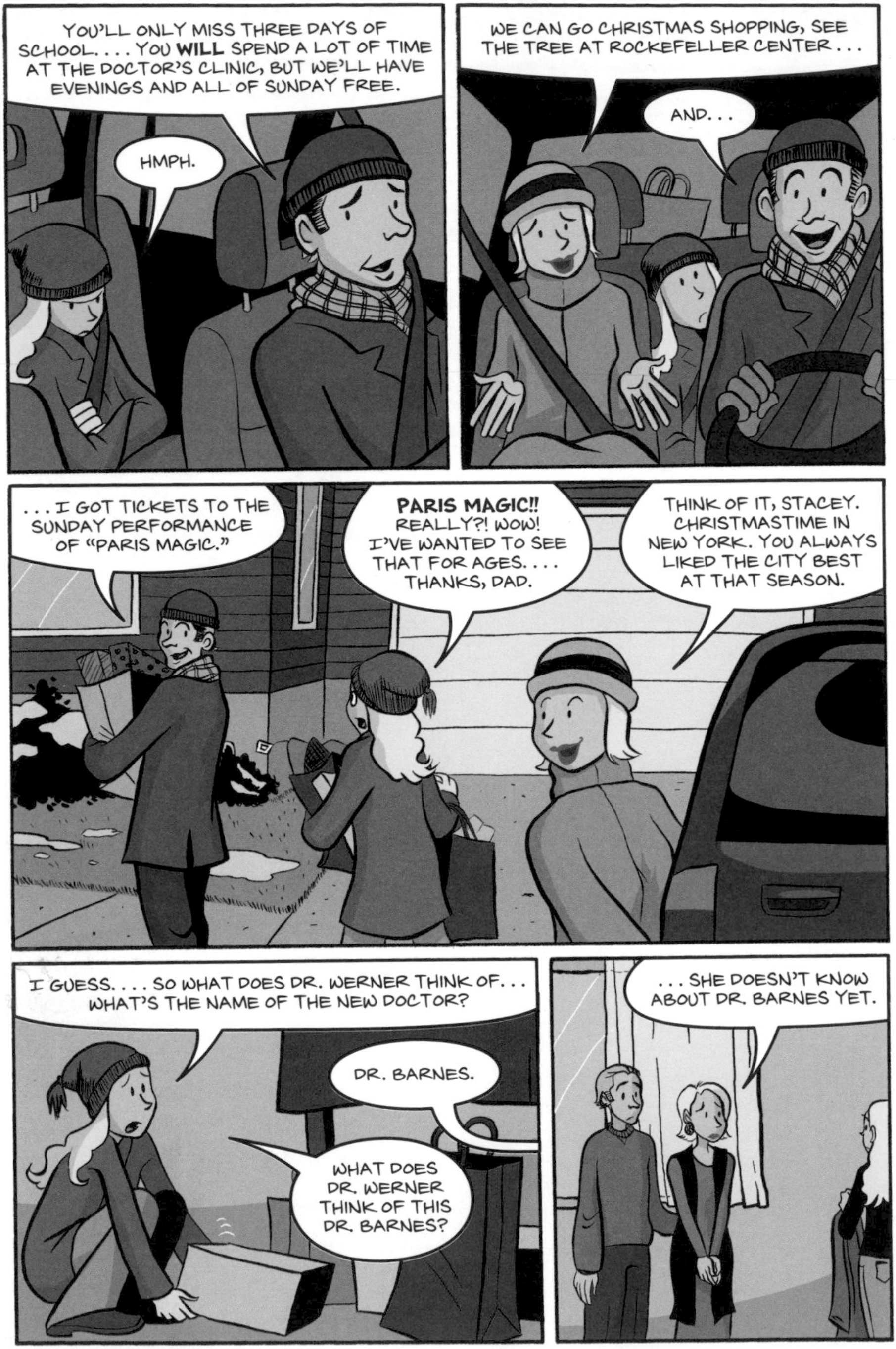
YOU'LL ONLY MISS THREE DAYS OF SCHOOL. . . . YOU **WILL** SPEND A LOT OF TIME AT THE DOCTOR'S CLINIC, BUT WE'LL HAVE EVENINGS AND ALL OF SUNDAY FREE.
HMPH.
WE CAN GO CHRISTMAS SHOPPING, SEE THE TREE AT ROCKEFELLER CENTER . . .
AND. . .
. . . I GOT TICKETS TO THE SUNDAY PERFORMANCE OF "PARIS MAGIC."
PARIS MAGIC!! REALLY?! WOW! I'VE WANTED TO SEE THAT FOR AGES. . . . THANKS, DAD.
THINK OF IT, STACEY. CHRISTMASTIME IN NEW YORK. YOU ALWAYS LIKED THE CITY BEST AT THAT SEASON.
I GUESS. . . . SO WHAT DOES DR. WERNER THINK OF. . . WHAT'S THE NAME OF THE NEW DOCTOR?
DR. BARNES.
WHAT DOES DR. WERNER THINK OF THIS DR. BARNES?
. . . SHE DOESN'T KNOW ABOUT DR. BARNES YET.

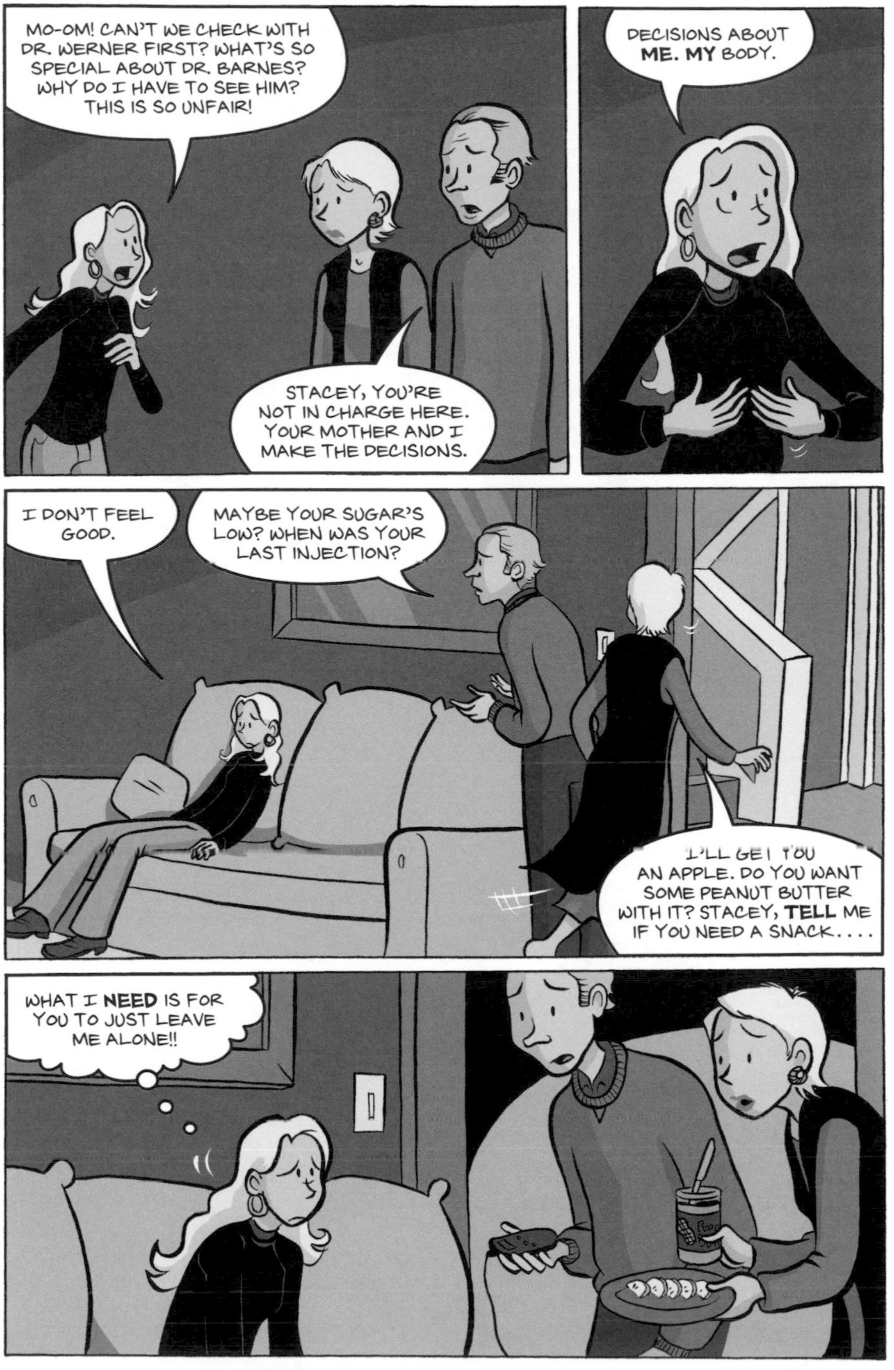
MO-OM! CAN'T WE CHECK WITH DR. WERNER FIRST? WHAT'S SO SPECIAL ABOUT DR. BARNES? WHY DO I HAVE TO SEE HIM? THIS IS SO UNFAIR!
STACEY, YOU'RE NOT IN CHARGE HERE. YOUR MOTHER AND I MAKE THE DECISIONS.
DECISIONS ABOUT **ME. MY** BODY.
I DON'T FEEL GOOD.
MAYBE YOUR SUGAR'S LOW? WHEN WAS YOUR LAST INJECTION?
I'LL GET YOU AN APPLE. DO YOU WANT SOME PEANUT BUTTER WITH IT? STACEY, **TELL** ME IF YOU NEED A SNACK....
WHAT I **NEED** IS FOR YOU TO JUST LEAVE ME ALONE!!

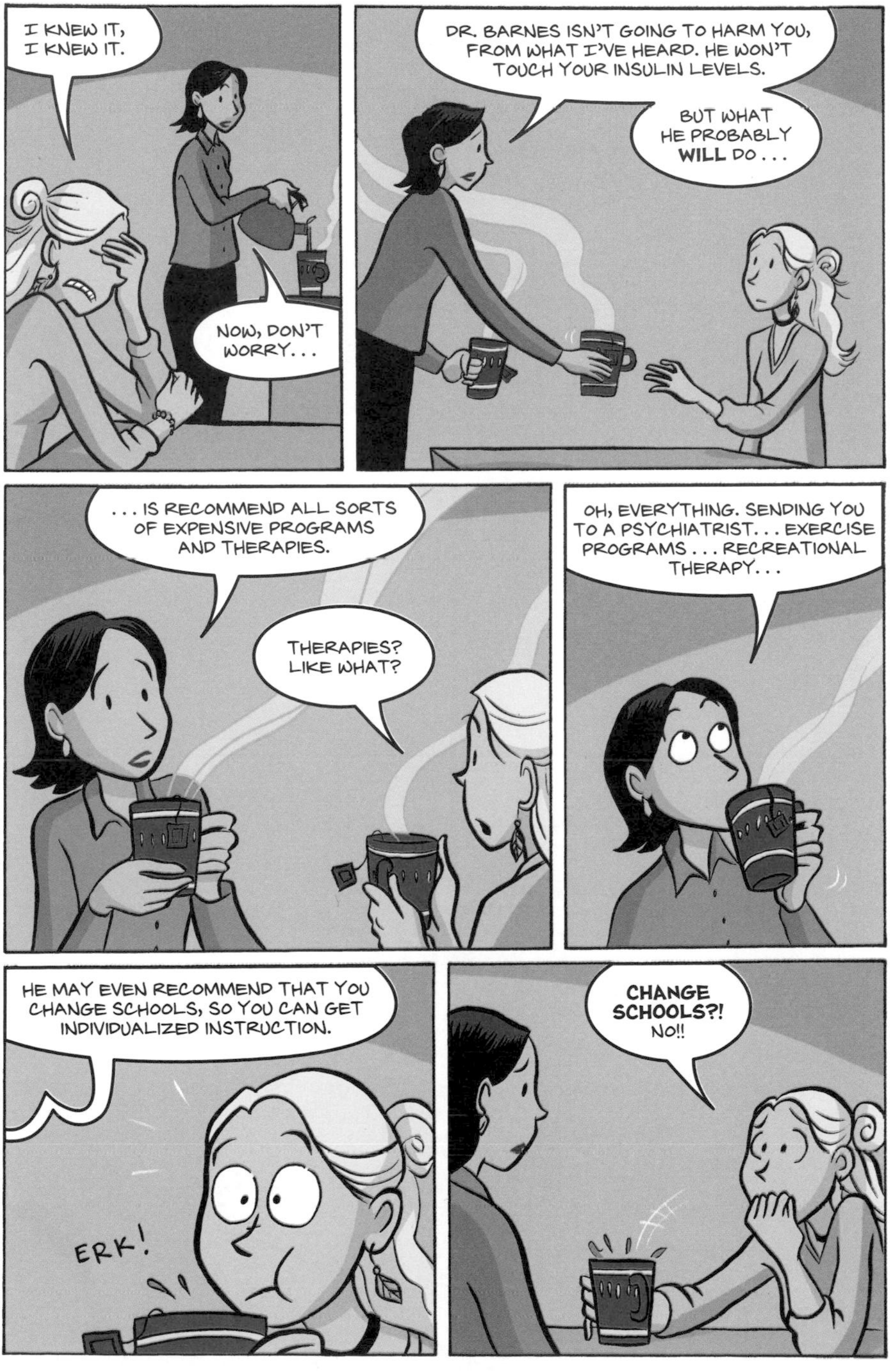
I KNEW IT, I KNEW IT.
NOW, DON'T WORRY. . .
DR. BARNES ISN'T GOING TO HARM YOU, FROM WHAT I'VE HEARD. HE WON'T TOUCH YOUR INSULIN LEVELS.
BUT WHAT HE PROBABLY **WILL** DO . . .
. . . IS RECOMMEND ALL SORTS OF EXPENSIVE PROGRAMS AND THERAPIES.
THERAPIES? LIKE WHAT?
OH, EVERYTHING. SENDING YOU TO A PSYCHIATRIST. . . EXERCISE PROGRAMS . . . RECREATIONAL THERAPY. . .
HE MAY EVEN RECOMMEND THAT YOU CHANGE SCHOOLS, SO YOU CAN GET INDIVIDUALIZED INSTRUCTION.
ERK!
CHANGE SCHOOLS?! NO!!

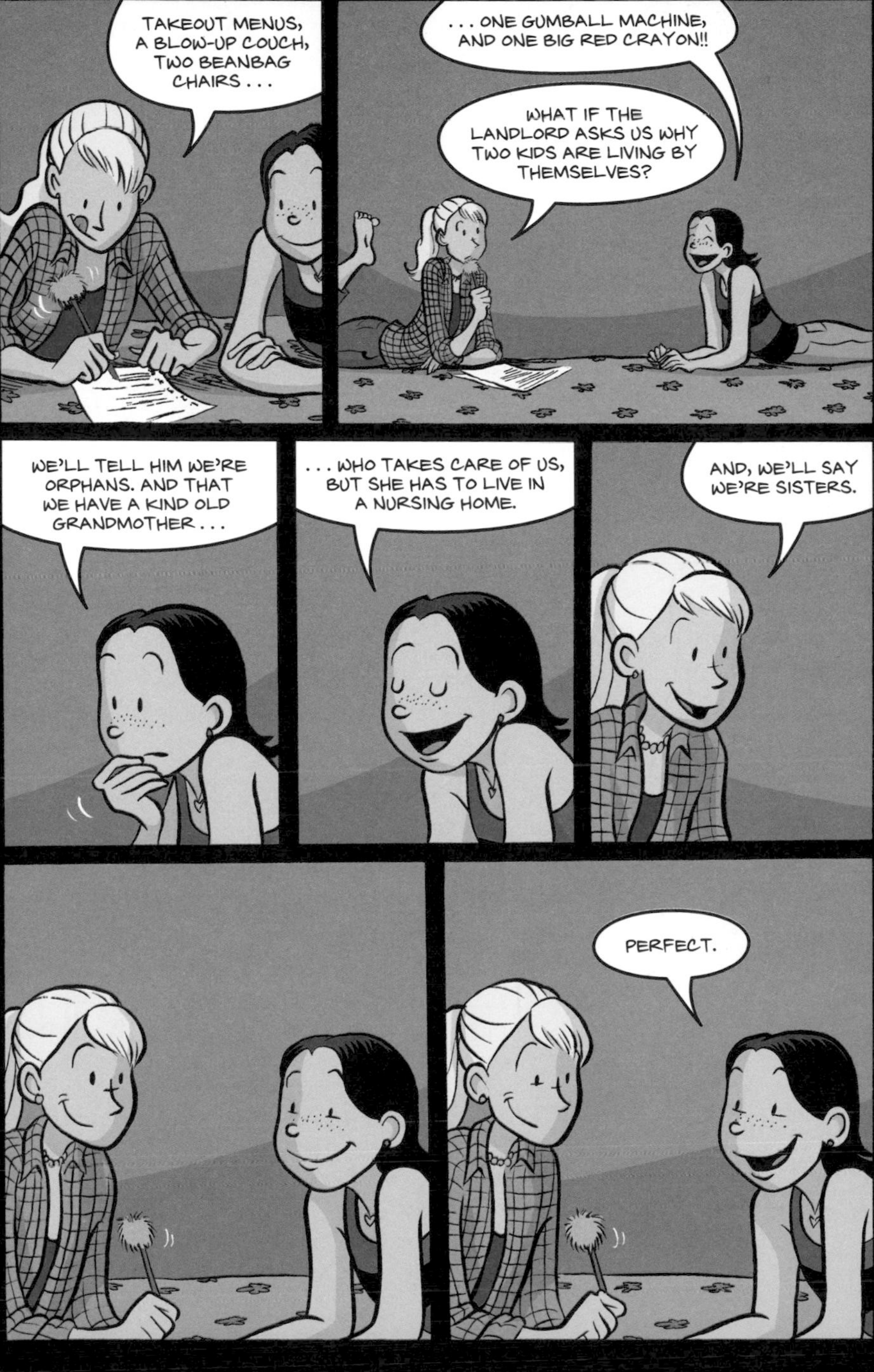
TAKEOUT MENUS, A BLOW-UP COUCH, TWO BEANBAG CHAIRS . . .
. . . ONE GUMBALL MACHINE, AND ONE BIG RED CRAYON!!
WHAT IF THE LANDLORD ASKS US WHY TWO KIDS ARE LIVING BY THEMSELVES?
WE'LL TELL HIM WE'RE ORPHANS. AND THAT WE HAVE A KIND OLD GRANDMOTHER . . .
. . . WHO TAKES CARE OF US, BUT SHE HAS TO LIVE IN A NURSING HOME.
AND, WE'LL SAY WE'RE SISTERS.
PERFECT.

CHAPTER 8

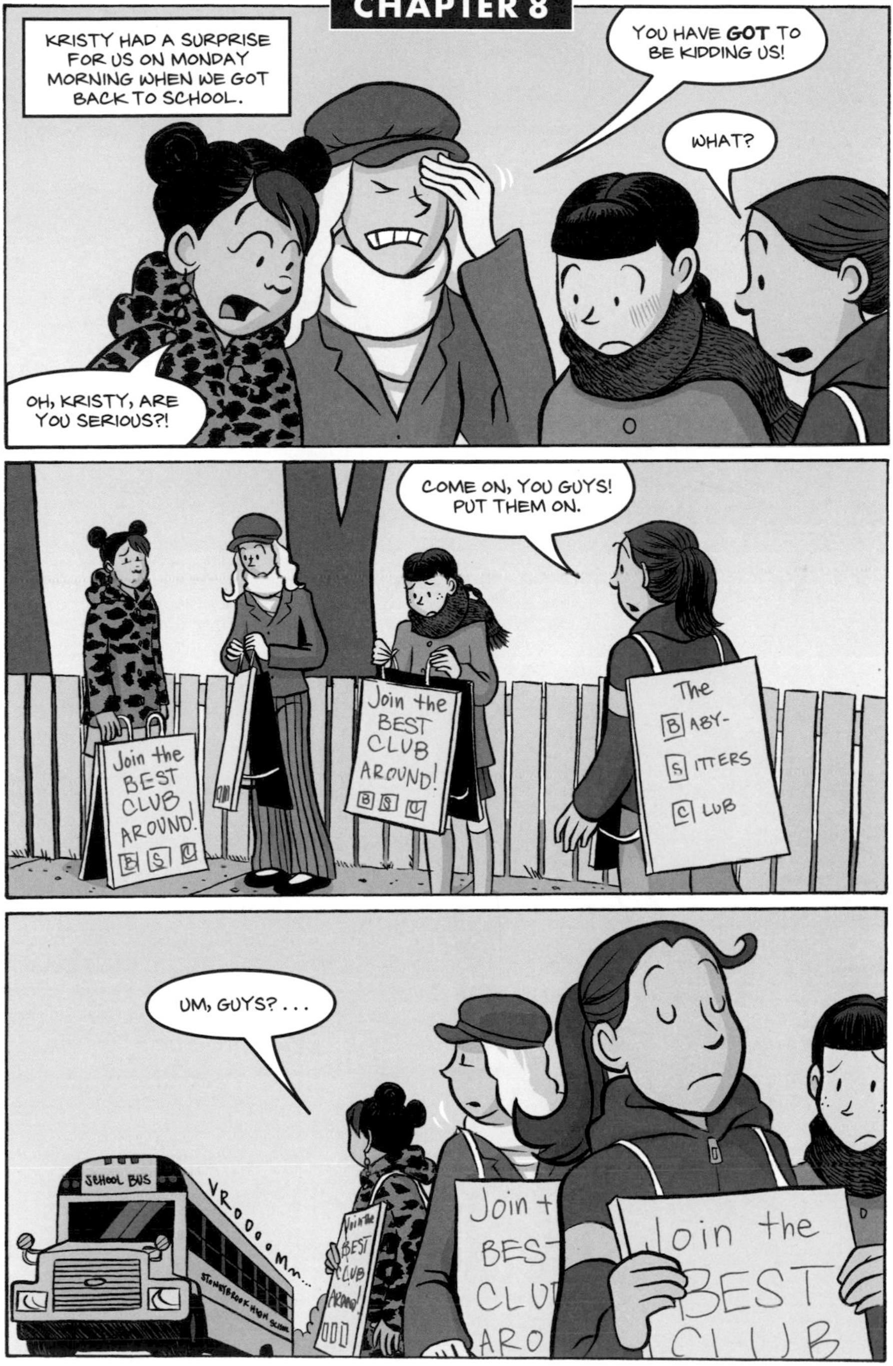

KRISTY HAD A SURPRISE FOR US ON MONDAY MORNING WHEN WE GOT BACK TO SCHOOL.
OH, KRISTY, ARE YOU SERIOUS?!
YOU HAVE **GOT** TO BE KIDDING US!
WHAT?
COME ON, YOU GUYS! PUT THEM ON.
Join the BEST CLUB AROUND! BSC
Join the BEST CLUB AROUND! BSC
The BABY-SITTERS CLUB
UM, GUYS? . . .
SCHOOL BUS
VROOOOOMM...
STONEYBROOK HIGH SCHOOL
Join the BEST CLUB AROUND!

WOOO!

HEY, GIRLS! GIMME YOUR NUMBER--I MIGHT NEED A SITTER!

HEY, HEY!

OKAY, WE SHOULD SPREAD OUT NOW.

YOU MEAN WE HAVE TO DO THIS **ALONE?!**

The B ABY-S ITTERS C LUB

The B ABY-S ITTERS C LUB

The B ABY-S ITTERS C LUB

The B ABY-S ITTERS C LUB

WHAT'S THE BABY-SITTERS CLUB?

Join The BEST CLUB AROUND!

OH, IT'S GREAT! WE GET LOTS OF JOBS. WE MEET THREE TIMES A WEEK TO . . .

Join th BEST CLU

YOU HAVE TO GO TO THREE MEETINGS A WEEK? I'M TOO BUSY FOR THAT.

Join The BEST CLUB AROUND

THAT SOUNDS LIKE TOO MUCH WORK.

I DON'T REALLY LIKE KIDS.

FRESH

MY GRANDMA BABY-SITS **ME** ALL THE TIME.

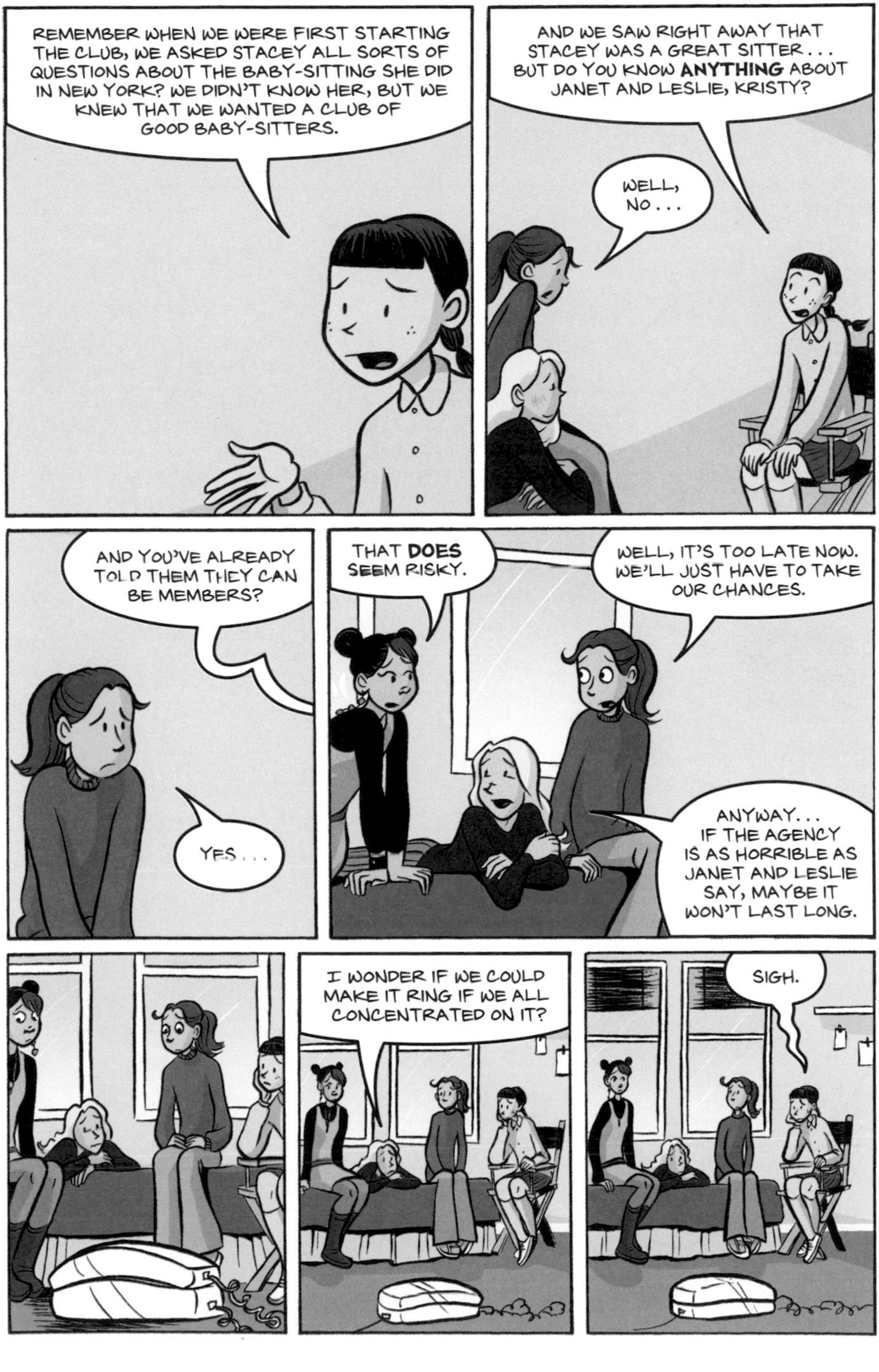
REMEMBER WHEN WE WERE FIRST STARTING THE CLUB, WE ASKED STACEY ALL SORTS OF QUESTIONS ABOUT THE BABY-SITTING SHE DID IN NEW YORK? WE DIDN'T KNOW HER, BUT WE KNEW THAT WE WANTED A CLUB OF GOOD BABY-SITTERS.
AND WE SAW RIGHT AWAY THAT STACEY WAS A GREAT SITTER . . . BUT DO YOU KNOW **ANYTHING** ABOUT JANET AND LESLIE, KRISTY?
WELL, NO . . .
AND YOU'VE ALREADY TOLD THEM THEY CAN BE MEMBERS?
YES . . .
THAT **DOES** SEEM RISKY.
WELL, IT'S TOO LATE NOW. WE'LL JUST HAVE TO TAKE OUR CHANCES.
ANYWAY. . . IF THE AGENCY IS AS HORRIBLE AS JANET AND LESLIE SAY, MAYBE IT WON'T LAST LONG.
I WONDER IF WE COULD MAKE IT RING IF WE ALL CONCENTRATED ON IT?
SIGH.

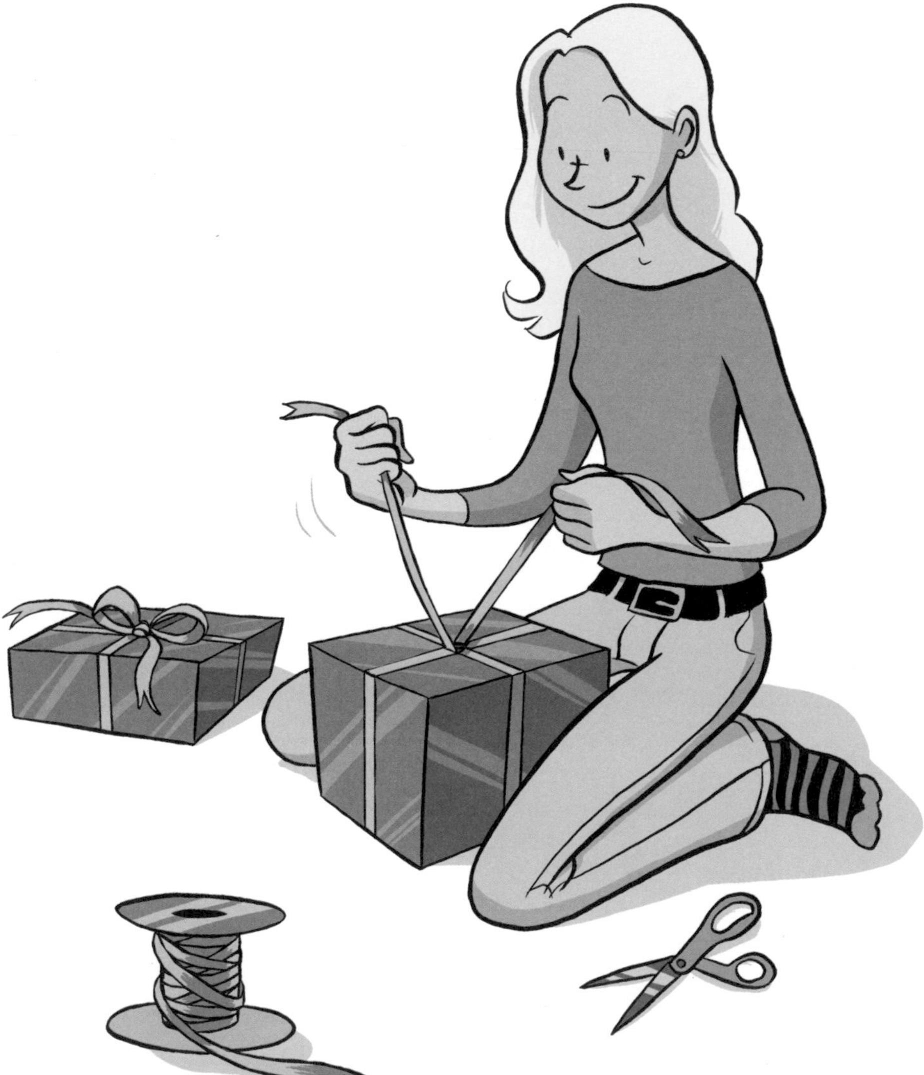

75

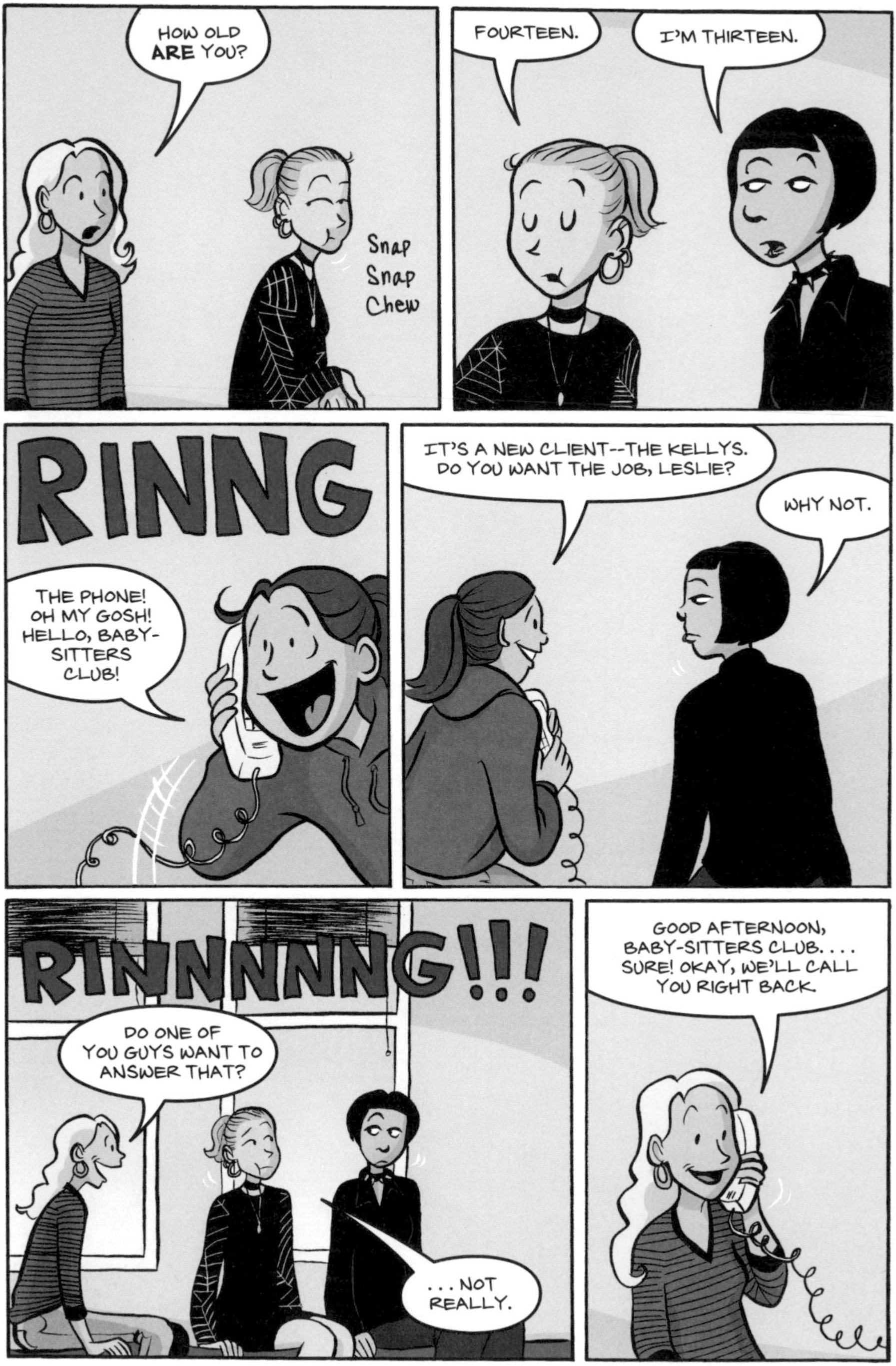

HOW OLD ARE YOU?
Snap Snap Chew
FOURTEEN.
I'M THIRTEEN.
RINNG
THE PHONE! OH MY GOSH! HELLO, BABY-SITTERS CLUB!
IT'S A NEW CLIENT--THE KELLYS. DO YOU WANT THE JOB, LESLIE?
WHY NOT.
RINNNNNG!!!
DO ONE OF YOU GUYS WANT TO ANSWER THAT?
. . . NOT REALLY.
GOOD AFTERNOON, BABY-SITTERS CLUB. . . . SURE! OKAY, WE'LL CALL YOU RIGHT BACK.

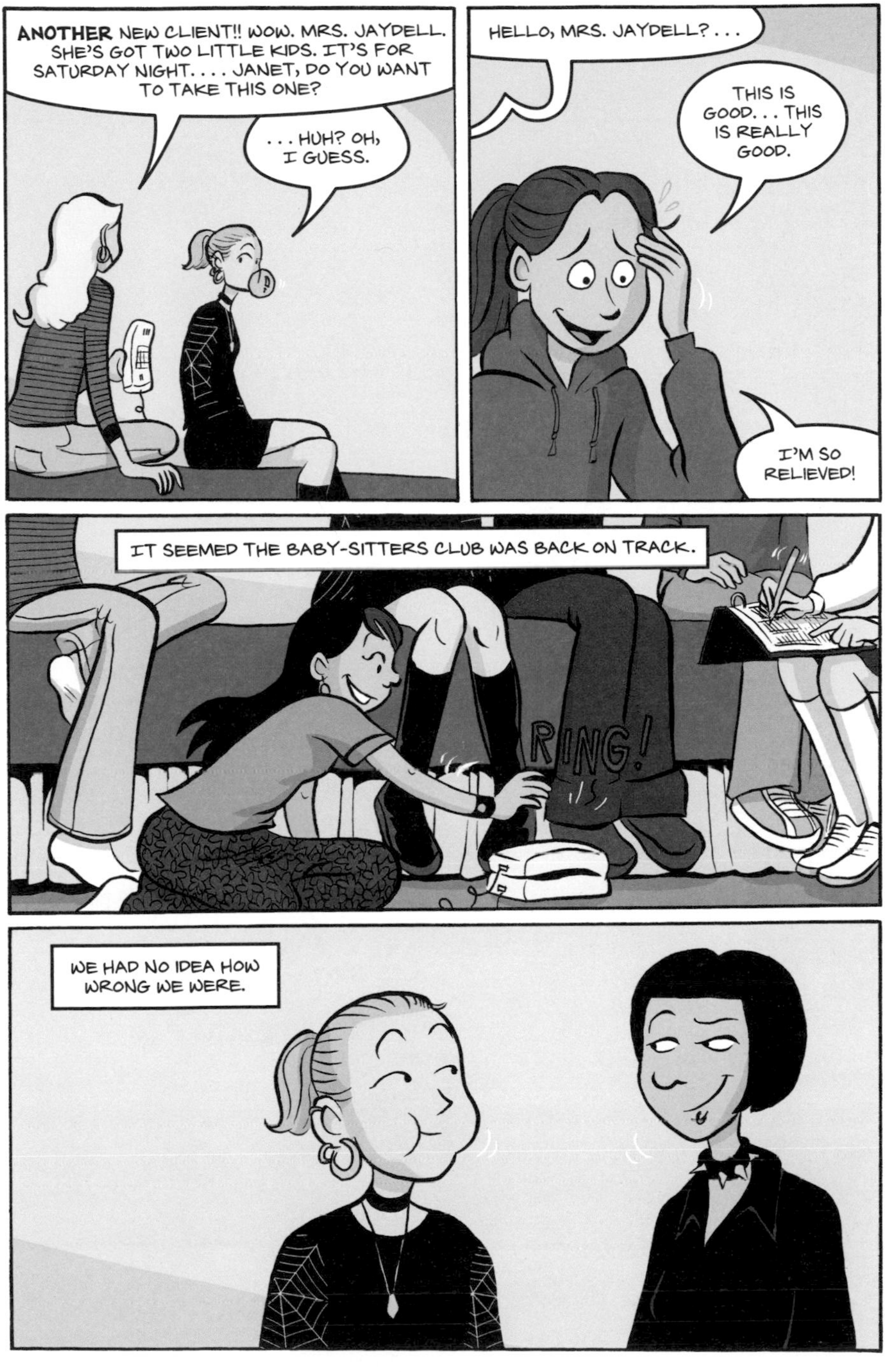
ANOTHER NEW CLIENT!! WOW. MRS. JAYDELL. SHE'S GOT TWO LITTLE KIDS. IT'S FOR SATURDAY NIGHT. . . . JANET, DO YOU WANT TO TAKE THIS ONE?
. . . HUH? OH, I GUESS.
HELLO, MRS. JAYDELL? . . .
THIS IS GOOD. . . THIS IS REALLY GOOD.
I'M SO RELIEVED!
IT SEEMED THE BABY-SITTERS CLUB WAS BACK ON TRACK.
RING!
WE HAD NO IDEA HOW WRONG WE WERE.

Monday, December 8

Today Kristy, Stacey + Mary Anne all
arived early for our baby-sitters club
meeting. We were all realy excited to find
out how Janet and Leslie's siting jobs
had gone on ~~too~~ Saturday.

When it was 5:30 we kept expecting the
doorbell to ring any seconde. But it
didnt. Soon it was 5:50. Where were
they. Krist was getting worried. ~~Writ~~ Write
this down in our notebook, somebody,
she said. Somethings wrong.

* Claudia *

CHAPTER 10

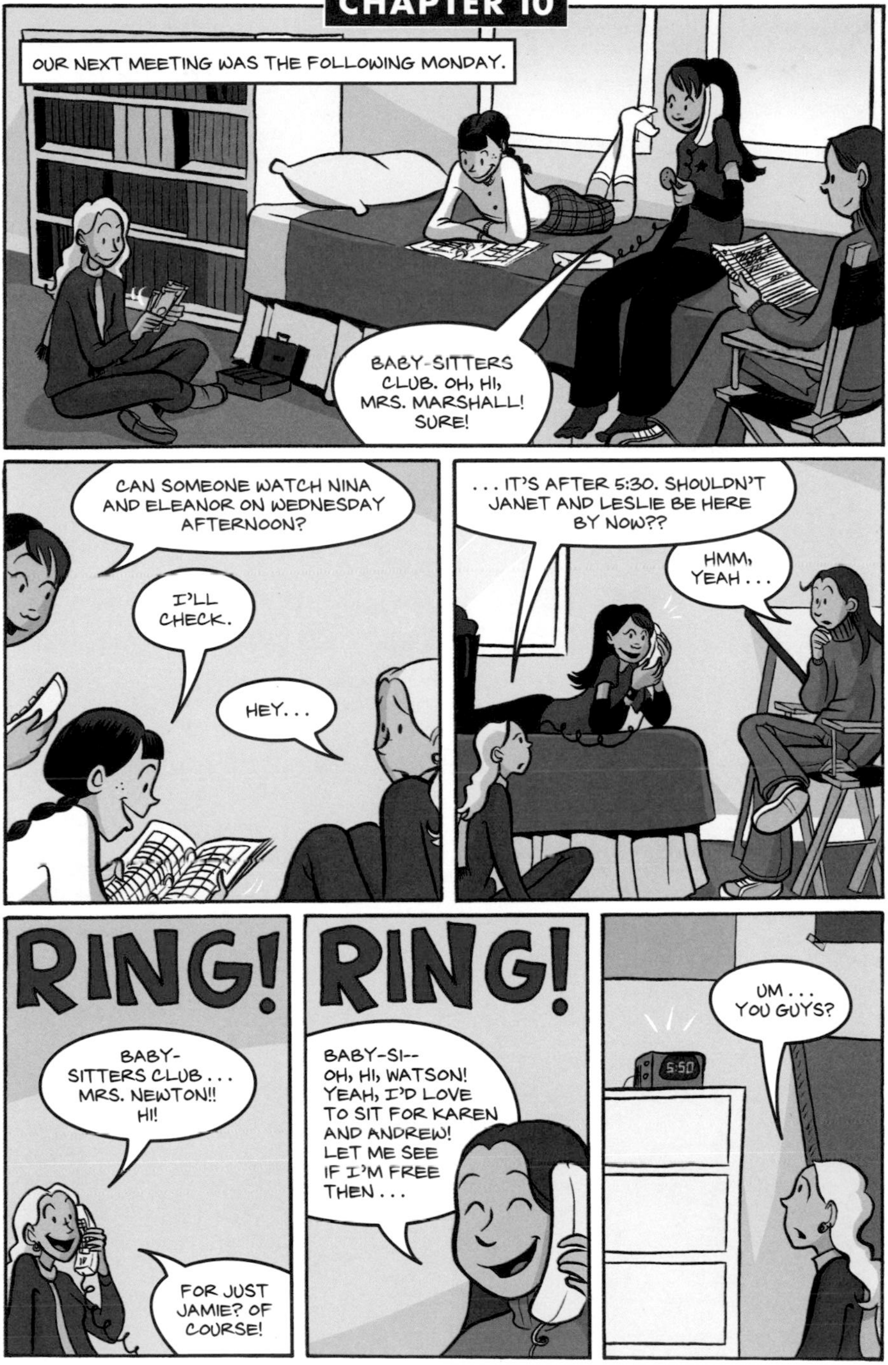
OUR NEXT MEETING WAS THE FOLLOWING MONDAY.
BABY-SITTERS CLUB. OH, HI, MRS. MARSHALL! SURE!
CAN SOMEONE WATCH NINA AND ELEANOR ON WEDNESDAY AFTERNOON?
I'LL CHECK.
HEY...
...IT'S AFTER 5:30. SHOULDN'T JANET AND LESLIE BE HERE BY NOW??
HMM, YEAH...
RING!
BABY-SITTERS CLUB... MRS. NEWTON!! HI!
FOR JUST JAMIE? OF COURSE!
RING!
BABY-SI-- OH, HI, WATSON! YEAH, I'D LOVE TO SIT FOR KAREN AND ANDREW! LET ME SEE IF I'M FREE THEN...
5:50
UM... YOU GUYS?

81

Wednesday, December 10th

Earlier this afternoon, I baby-sat for Jamie
while Mrs. Newton took Lucy to a doctor's
appointment. Something was bothering him. He
moped around as if he'd lost his best friend.
He greeted me cheerfully enough when I
arrived, but as soon as Mrs. Newton carried
a bundled-up Lucy out the back door, his
face fell....

Mary Anne

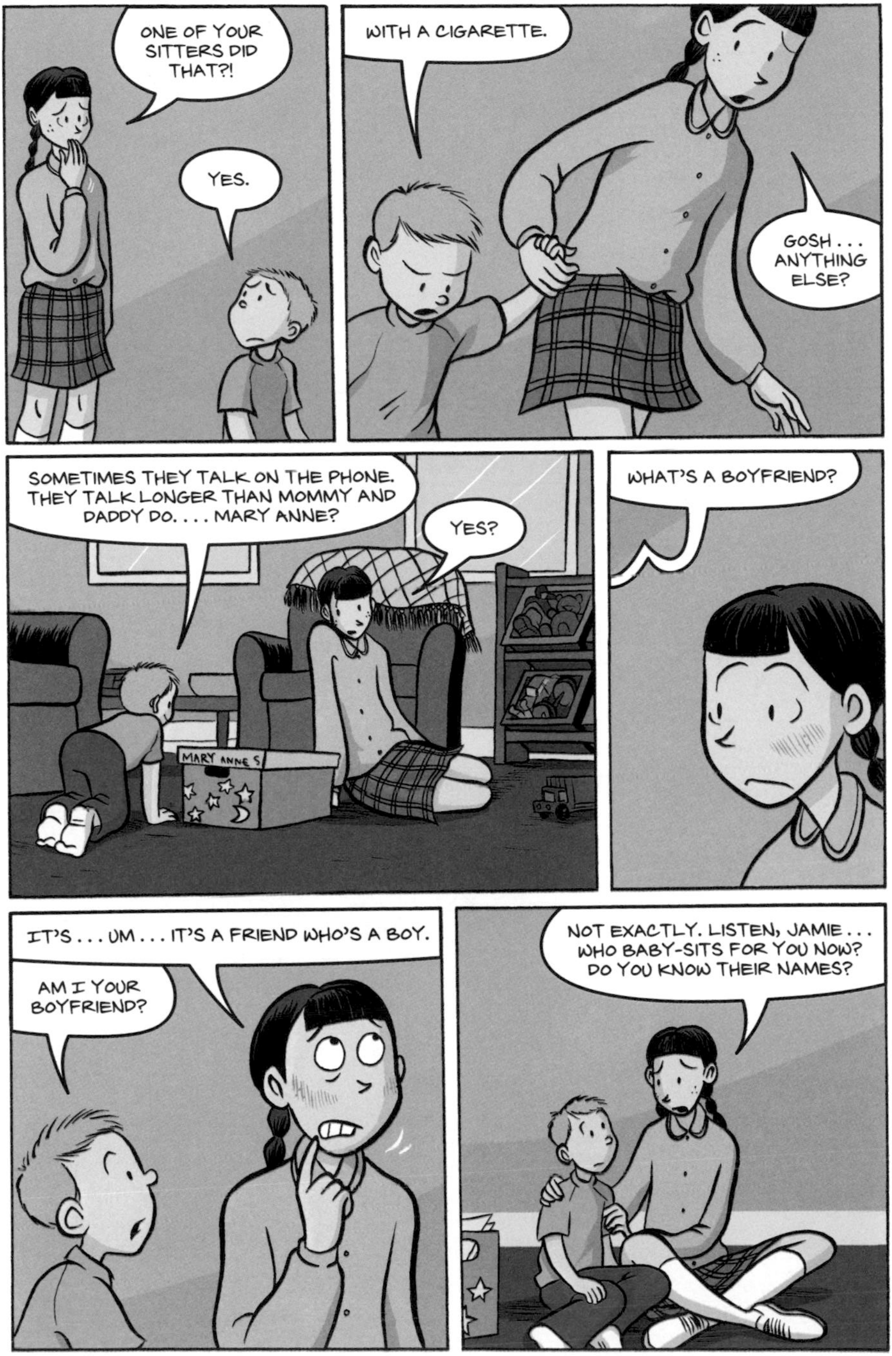

ONE OF YOUR SITTERS DID THAT?!
YES.
WITH A CIGARETTE.
GOSH . . . ANYTHING ELSE?
SOMETIMES THEY TALK ON THE PHONE. THEY TALK LONGER THAN MOMMY AND DADDY DO. . . . MARY ANNE?
YES?
MARY ANNE'S
WHAT'S A BOYFRIEND?
IT'S . . . UM . . . IT'S A FRIEND WHO'S A BOY.
AM I YOUR BOYFRIEND?
NOT EXACTLY. LISTEN, JAMIE . . . WHO BABY-SITS FOR YOU NOW? DO YOU KNOW THEIR NAMES?

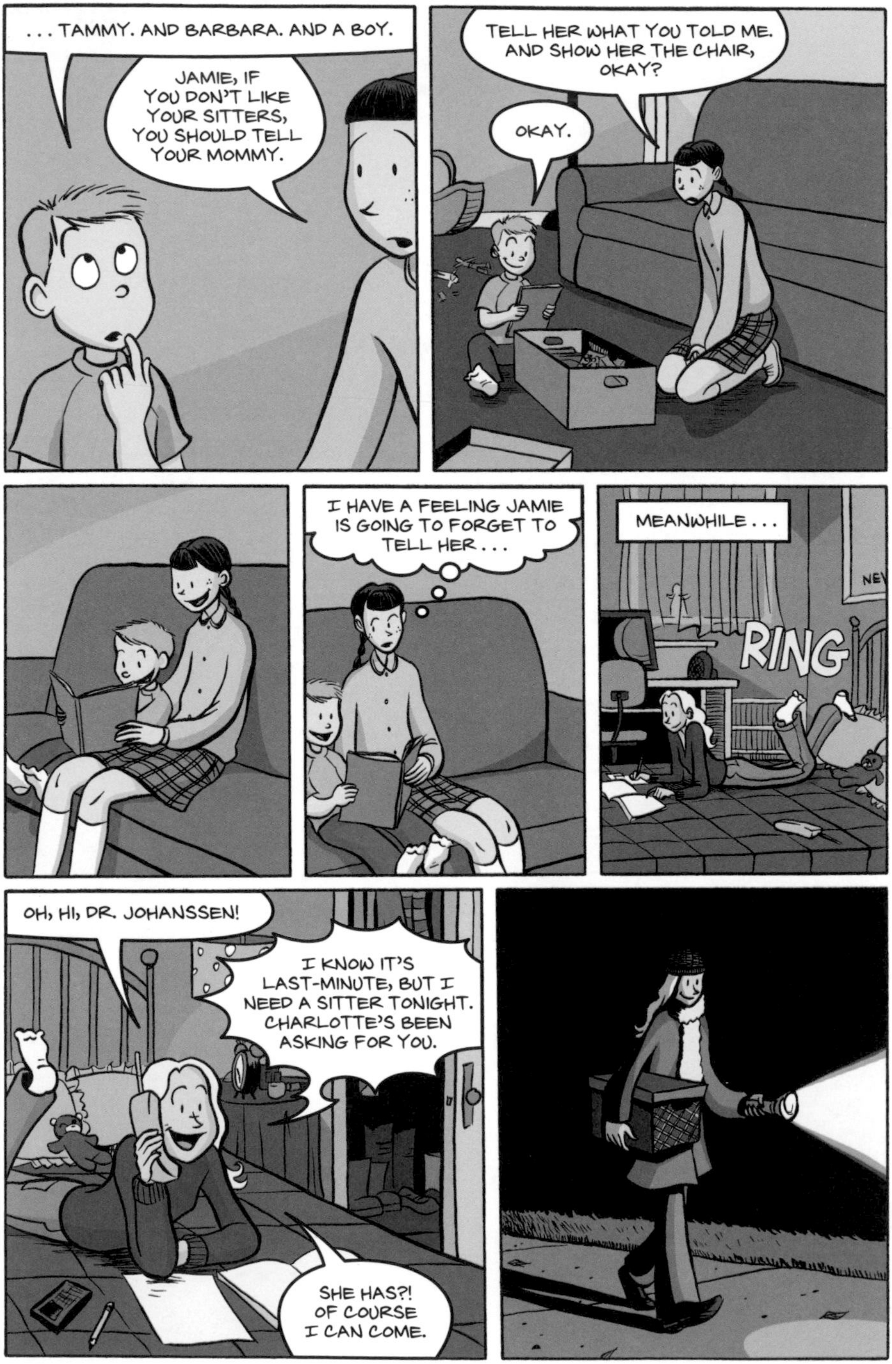
. . . TAMMY. AND BARBARA. AND A BOY.
JAMIE, IF YOU DON'T LIKE YOUR SITTERS, YOU SHOULD TELL YOUR MOMMY.
TELL HER WHAT YOU TOLD ME. AND SHOW HER THE CHAIR, OKAY?
OKAY.
I HAVE A FEELING JAMIE IS GOING TO FORGET TO TELL HER . . .
MEANWHILE . . .
RING
OH, HI, DR. JOHANSSEN!
I KNOW IT'S LAST-MINUTE, BUT I NEED A SITTER TONIGHT. CHARLOTTE'S BEEN ASKING FOR YOU.
SHE HAS?! OF COURSE I CAN COME.

102

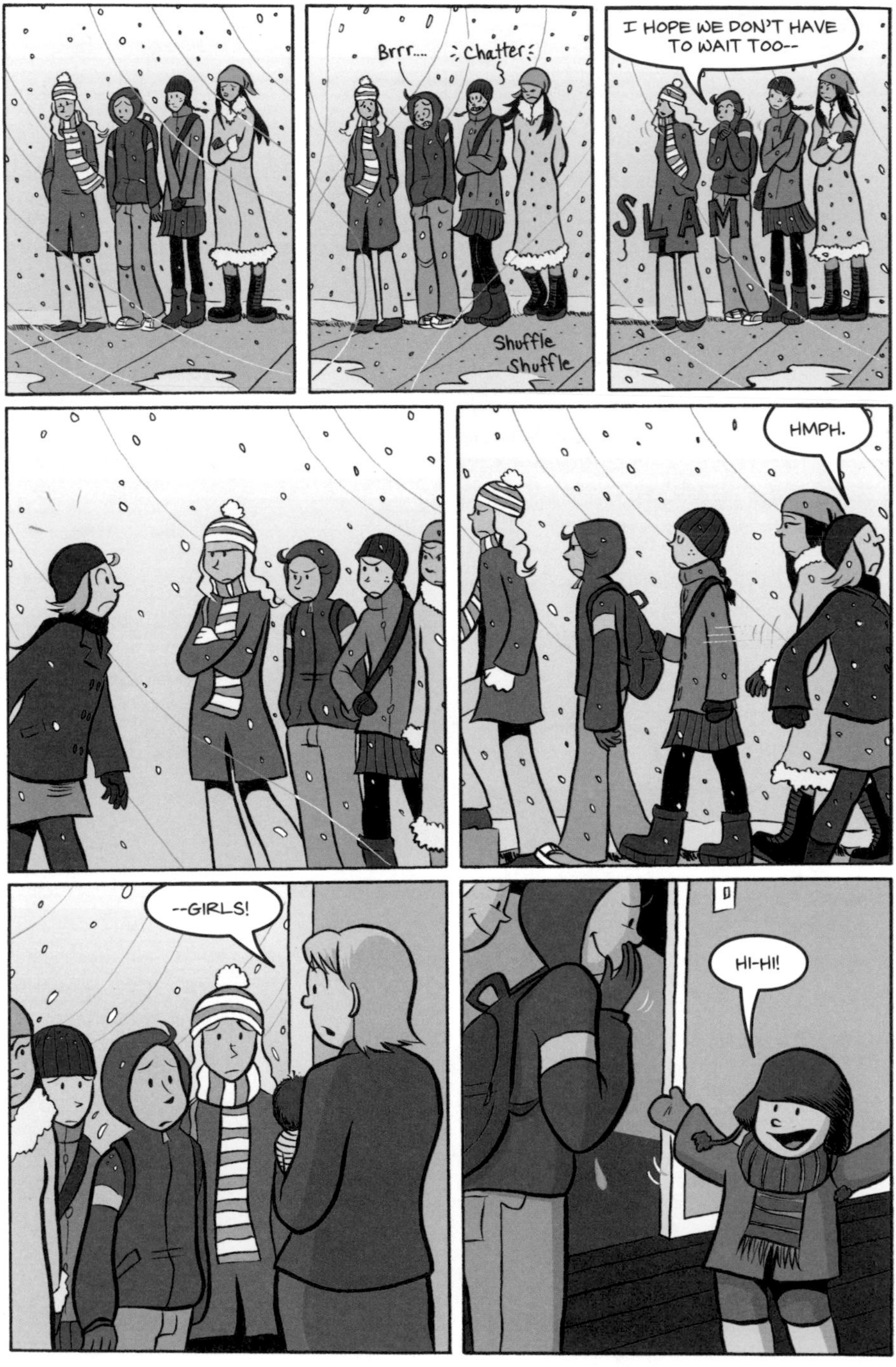
Brrr...
Chatter
Shuffle
Shuffle
I HOPE WE DON'T HAVE TO WAIT TOO--
SLAM
HMPH.
--GIRLS!
HI-HI!

105

CHAPTER 13

110

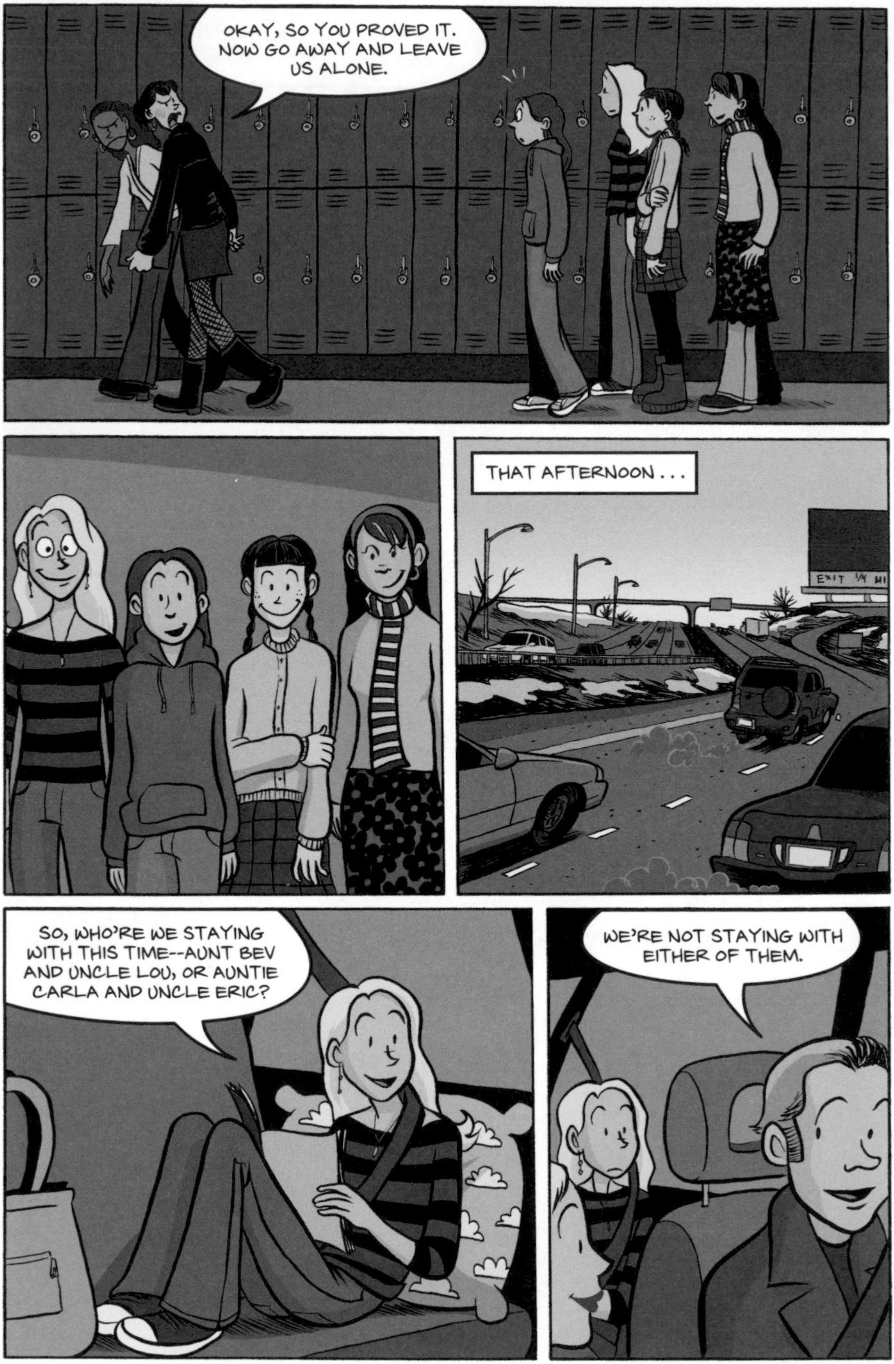
OKAY, SO YOU PROVED IT. NOW GO AWAY AND LEAVE US ALONE.
THAT AFTERNOON . . .
EXIT 1/4 MI
SO, WHO'RE WE STAYING WITH THIS TIME--AUNT BEV AND UNCLE LOU, OR AUNTIE CARLA AND UNCLE ERIC?
WE'RE NOT STAYING WITH EITHER OF THEM.

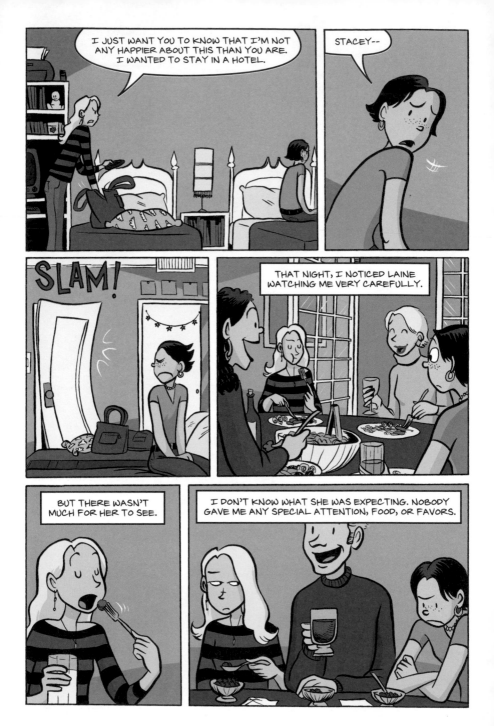

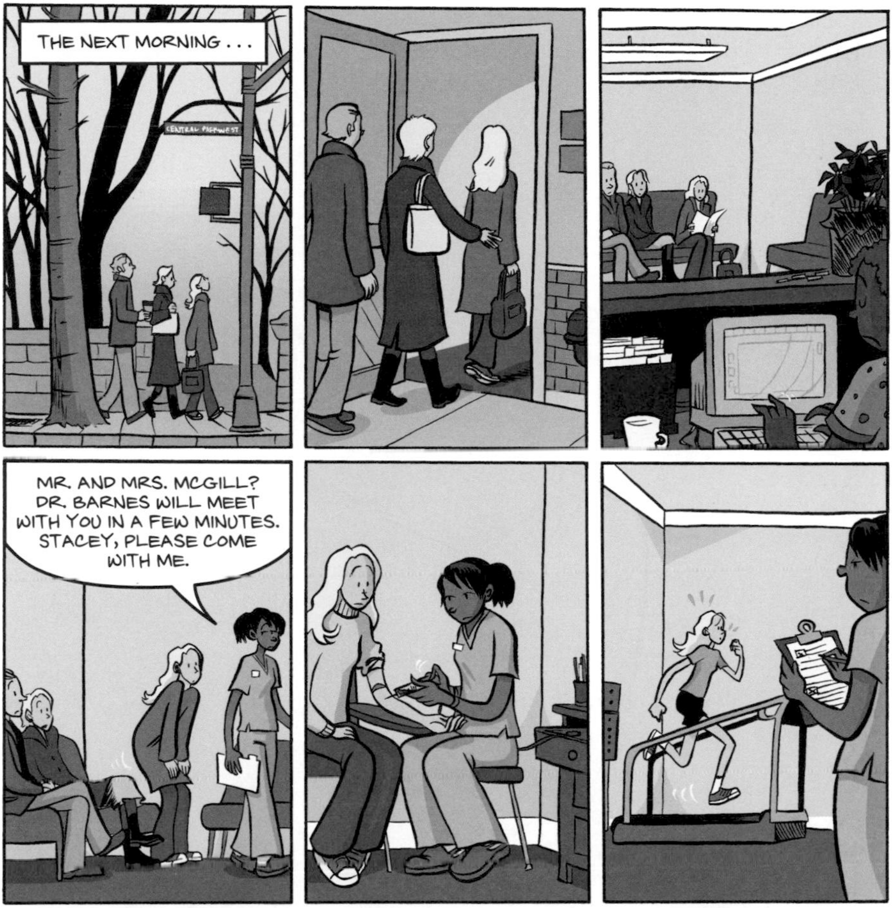
THE NEXT MORNING . . .
MR. AND MRS. MCGILL? DR. BARNES WILL MEET WITH YOU IN A FEW MINUTES. STACEY, PLEASE COME WITH ME.
?!

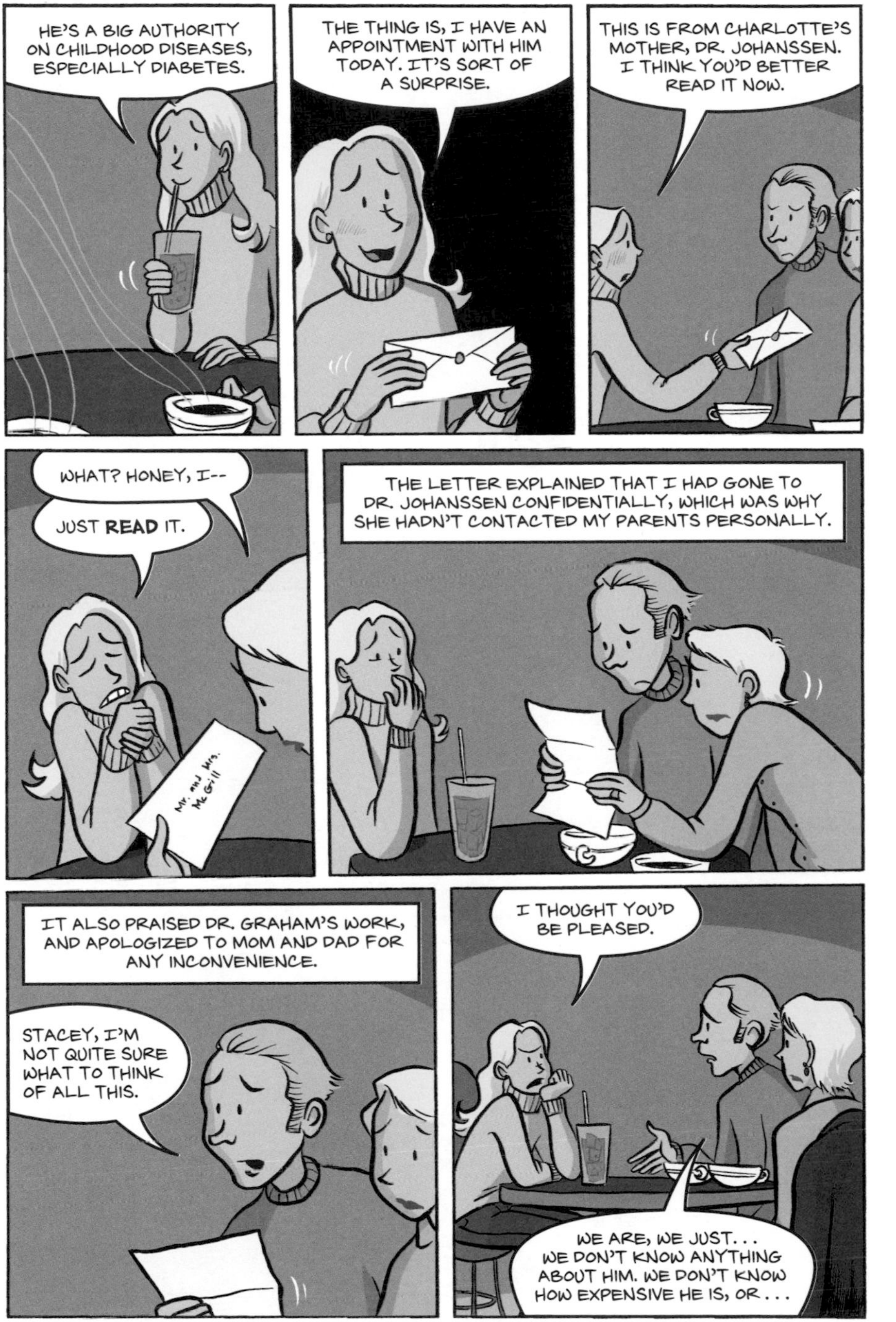
HE'S A BIG AUTHORITY ON CHILDHOOD DISEASES, ESPECIALLY DIABETES.
THE THING IS, I HAVE AN APPOINTMENT WITH HIM TODAY. IT'S SORT OF A SURPRISE.
THIS IS FROM CHARLOTTE'S MOTHER, DR. JOHANSSEN. I THINK YOU'D BETTER READ IT NOW.
WHAT? HONEY, I--
JUST **READ** IT.
Mr. and Mrs. McGill
THE LETTER EXPLAINED THAT I HAD GONE TO DR. JOHANSSEN CONFIDENTIALLY, WHICH WAS WHY SHE HADN'T CONTACTED MY PARENTS PERSONALLY.
IT ALSO PRAISED DR. GRAHAM'S WORK, AND APOLOGIZED TO MOM AND DAD FOR ANY INCONVENIENCE.
STACEY, I'M NOT QUITE SURE WHAT TO THINK OF ALL THIS.
I THOUGHT YOU'D BE PLEASED.
WE ARE, WE JUST. . . WE DON'T KNOW ANYTHING ABOUT HIM. WE DON'T KNOW HOW EXPENSIVE HE IS, OR . . .

120

CHAPTER 14

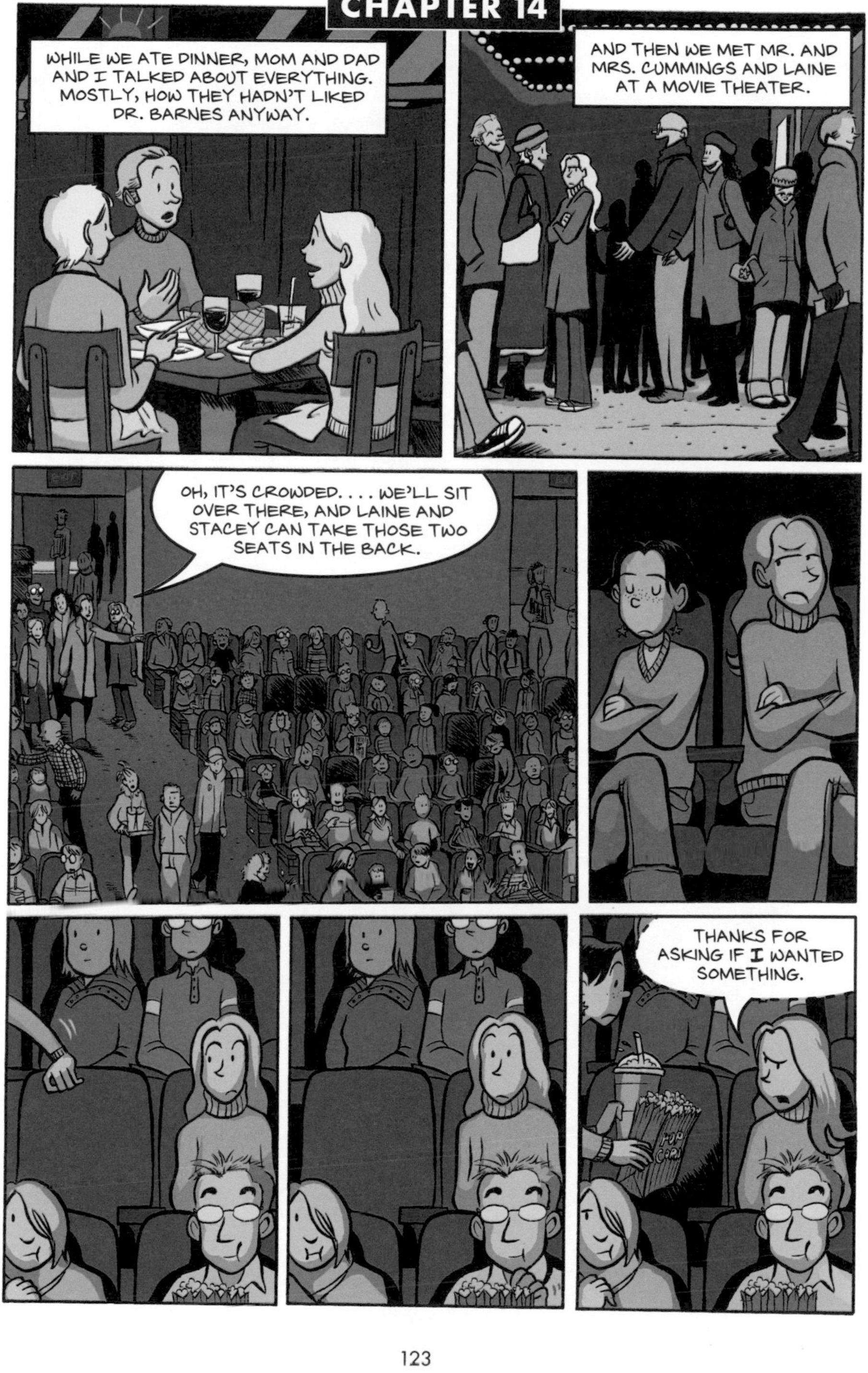
WHILE WE ATE DINNER, MOM AND DAD AND I TALKED ABOUT EVERYTHING. MOSTLY, HOW THEY HADN'T LIKED DR. BARNES ANYWAY.
AND THEN WE MET MR. AND MRS. CUMMINGS AND LAINE AT A MOVIE THEATER.
OH, IT'S CROWDED. . . . WE'LL SIT OVER THERE, AND LAINE AND STACEY CAN TAKE THOSE TWO SEATS IN THE BACK.
THANKS FOR ASKING IF I WANTED SOMETHING.

125

127

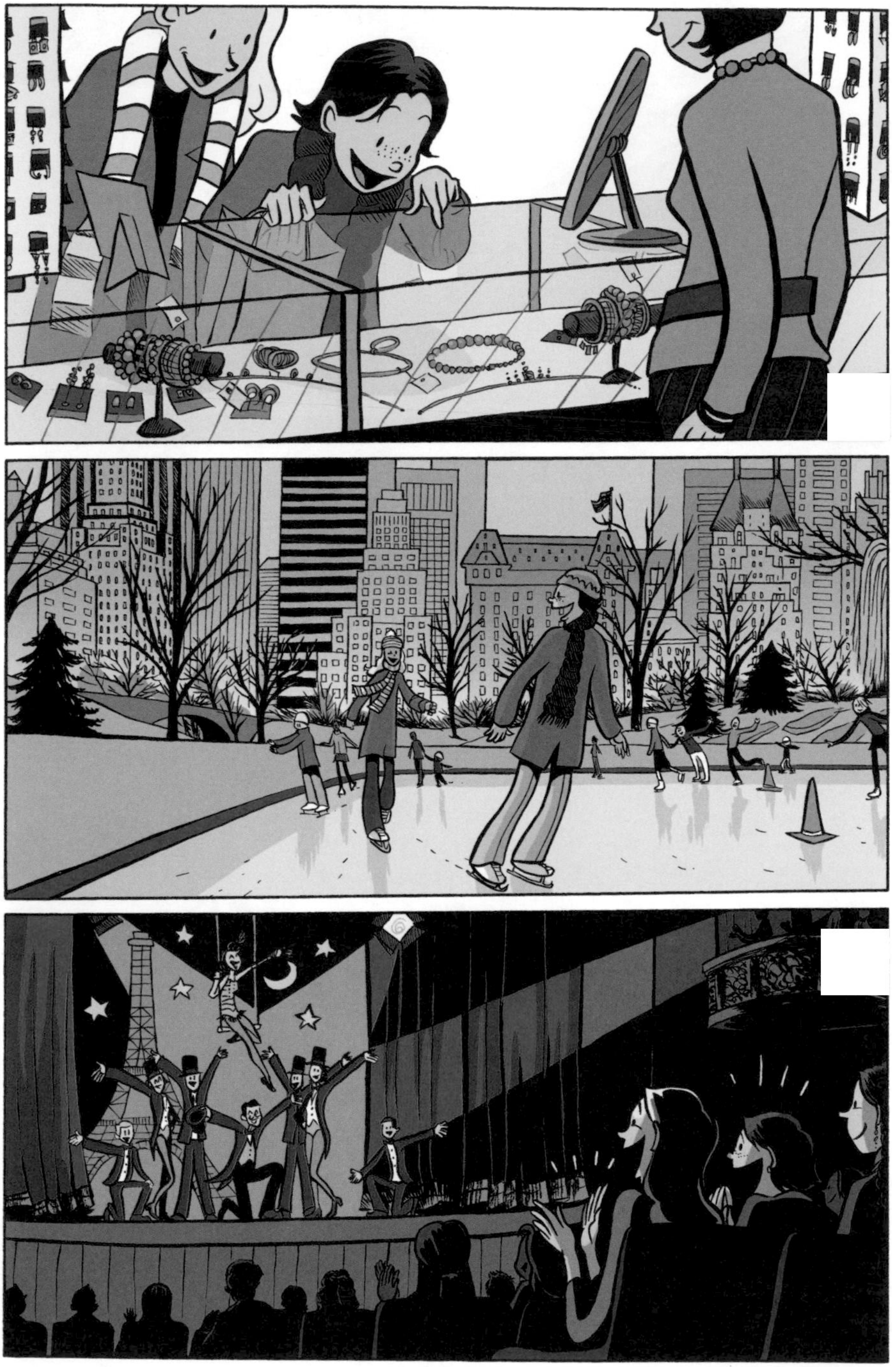

133

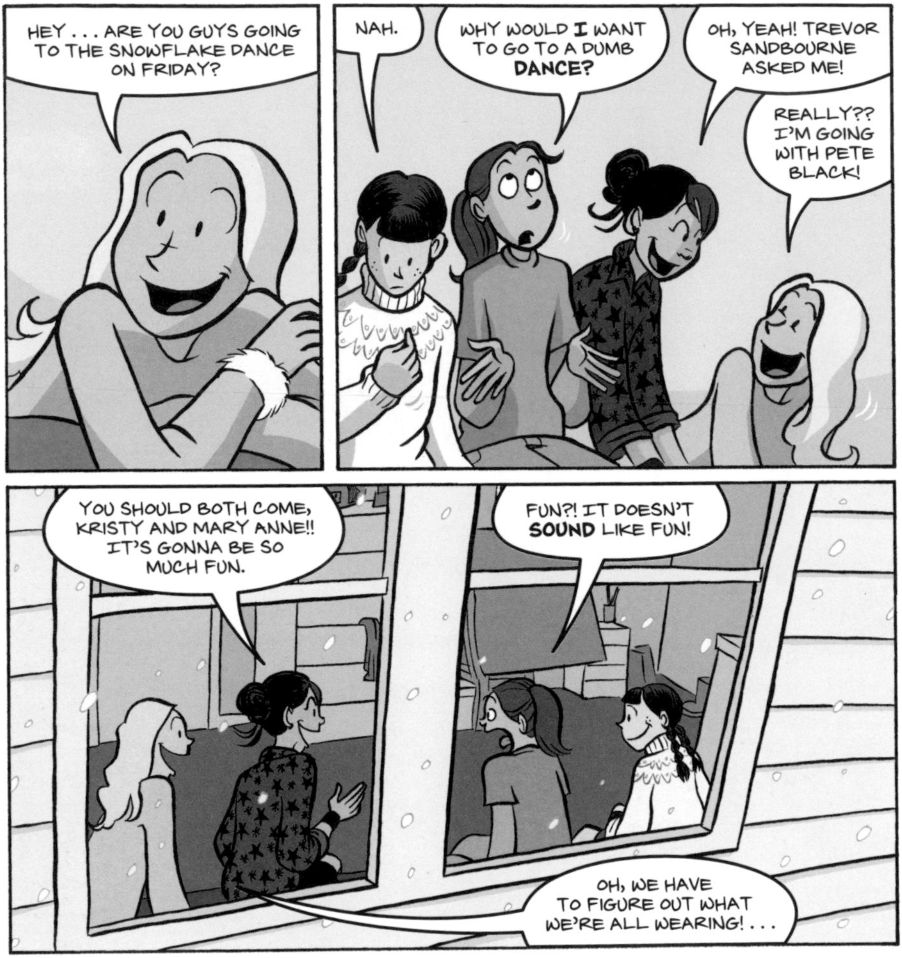
HEY . . . ARE YOU GUYS GOING TO THE SNOWFLAKE DANCE ON FRIDAY?
NAH.
WHY WOULD **I** WANT TO GO TO A DUMB **DANCE?**
OH, YEAH! TREVOR SANDBOURNE ASKED ME!
REALLY?? I'M GOING WITH PETE BLACK!
YOU SHOULD BOTH COME, KRISTY AND MARY ANNE!! IT'S GONNA BE SO MUCH FUN.
FUN?! IT DOESN'T **SOUND** LIKE FUN!
OH, WE HAVE TO FIGURE OUT WHAT WE'RE ALL WEARING! . . .

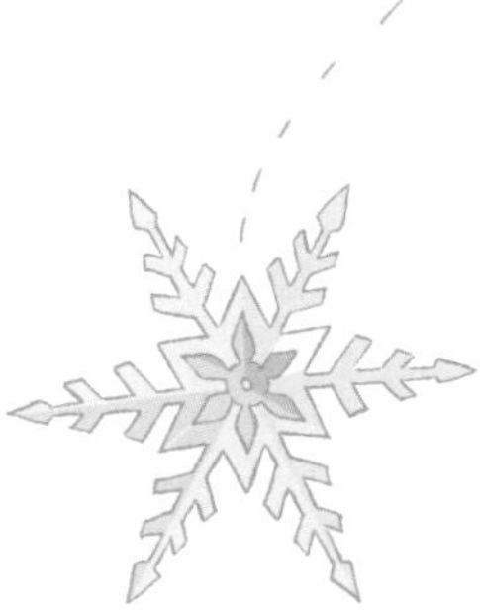

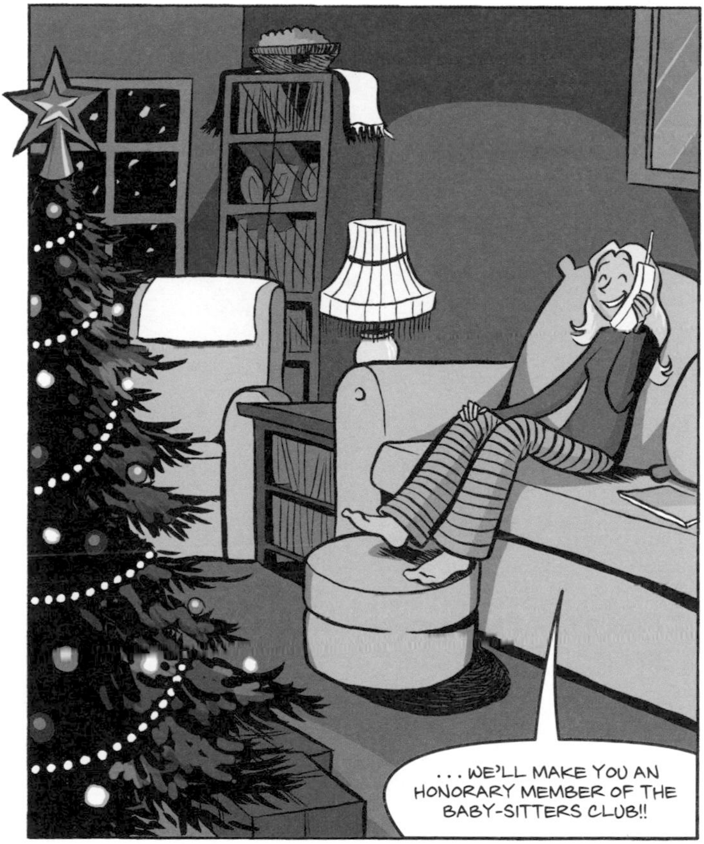

. . . WE'LL MAKE YOU AN HONORARY MEMBER OF THE BABY-SITTERS CLUB!!

This book is for my old pal, Claudia Werner
A. M. M.

Thanks to Marion Vitus, Adam Girardet, Duane Ballanger,
Lisa Jonte, Arthur Levine, and Braden Lamb. As always, a huge
thank-you to my family, my friends, and especially, Dave.
R. T.

Text copyright © 2006, 2015 by Ann M. Martin
Art copyright © 2006, 2015 by Raina Telgemeier

Library of Congress Control Number: 2014945627

ISBN 978-0-545-81388-4 (hardcover)
ISBN 978-0-545-81389-1 (paperback)

10 9 8 7 6 5 4 3 2 1   15 16 17 18 19

Printed in the U.S.A.   88
First color edition printing, August 2015

Lettering by John Green
Edited by David Levithan, Janna Morishima, and Cassandra Pelham
Book design by Phil Falco
Creative Director: David Saylor